WHITE CHRISTMAS

A CHRISTIAN MEDICAL ROMANCE

MONROE FAMILY
BOOK 6

LAURA SCOTT

1

———

Andrea Monroe stared grimly out the window of her patient's room. The snow was falling faster now, obliterating the view outside the surgical intensive care unit. Bad enough that she had to work Christmas Eve, not being home with her two kids, Bethany and Ben, who were staying with her parents and siblings, but what if she ended up stuck there overnight? With the way the snow was piling up outside, that was a distinct possibility.

Her husband had died eighteen months ago, forcing her to go back to work at Trinity Medical Center. This was her kids' second Christmas without their father. Not that they'd seemed to notice his absence. In truth, Stuart had traveled so much during their marriage that the kids hadn't missed him as much as she'd anticipated.

Andrea turned her attention back to her critically ill patient. Mr. Braun's breathing still wasn't good, and his oxygen saturation levels were dropping. She lifted a hand to the device around her neck to call the critical care fellow on duty when Dr. Noah Weston walked into the room.

"Hey, Andrea. He doesn't look any better," Noah observed.

"No, I'm afraid not." After working with Noah over the past six months, his fellowship started on July 1, she had learned to admire his skill and amazing bedside manner. "I was just going to page you. I know you prepared Mr. Braun for this possibility. Would you like me to get the intubation cart and ventilator?"

"I'll grab them. Keep an eye on him." Noah turned and left the room. This was another reason why she liked Noah. He didn't think fetching supplies for himself was beneath him.

Unlike some of the residents and attendings on duty.

Andrea leaned over the head of her patient's bed to make sure the suction equipment was ready to go. The monitor overhead began to alarm with the low saturation levels. She reached up to silence it, then adjusted the patient's non-rebreather face mask.

"Mr. Braun, we're going to help your breathing, okay?" His eyelids fluttered, but he didn't nod or acknowledge her statement. Maybe because he was already becoming too hypoxic to understand what was going on. "Dr. Weston will be here soon. He's going to put in that breathing tube you talked about."

Still no response. A niggle of concern snaked down her spine. Mr. Braun had recently undergone a bowel resection. That procedure didn't normally require ICU-level care, but Mr. Braun's lung status had been borderline. Now she was glad he was there to get the help he needed.

Despite being away from the bedside for almost four years, she'd managed to step right back in as if she'd never left. And in a way, she wished she'd kept her job rather than quitting to stay home with the kids. But that was in the past. All she could do now was move forward.

Noah wheeled the airway cart and ventilator into the room. A respiratory therapist accompanied him and began setting up the ventilator. She and Noah quickly removed the items they'd need to secure an emergency airway.

"What meds would you like me to give?" Andrea glanced at Noah.

"Ten of succinylcholine and five of midazolam." He flashed a smile. "Thanks."

She darted out of the room and strode quickly to the medication dispensing machine, which was how the nursing staff accessed emergency medications. Less than a minute later, she was back in Mr. Braun's room.

Noah already had the bed pulled away from the wall so he could position himself behind the patient's head. Drake, the respiratory therapist, stood off to one side. Andrea held the medications in her hand but didn't immediately give them. "We should do a time-out."

"Yes, we are going to place a size eight endotracheal tube in patient Kevin Braun. I'd like you to give him ten milligrams of succinylcholine and five milligrams of midazolam."

"Understood." She gave both medications via the IV catheter, then positioned herself on the other side to assist with the procedure. While Mr. Braun's oxygenation levels were dangerously low, placing a breathing tube was a routine procedure for the ICU.

Noah removed the patient's mask and quickly tipped his head back. Andrea stayed close with the suction, helping to keep her patient's airway clear. Noah used the laryngoscope to view the vocal cords, then reached for the endotracheal tube.

Within seconds, he slid the tube into place. "Let's check placement," Noah said.

Drake attached the color device to verify tube placement while Andrea used her stethoscope to listen for bilateral breath sounds. "Lung sounds are good on both sides."

"Color change to yellow indicates correct placement," Drake added.

"Great." Noah secured the tube in place. "I'll order a chest X-ray, too, to see what else is going on."

He'd barely said the words when the heart monitor began to alarm. Andrea glanced up to see her patient's heart rate had morphed from normal sinus rhythm into ventricular fibrillation.

"V-fib! We need the crash cart!" She lowered the head of the bed and pushed the button to firm up the air mattress to allow for possible chest compressions. Shocking with a defibrillator was the first course of treatment, but if that didn't work, they would need to perform CPR.

One of Andrea's colleagues, Gina, brought the crash cart into the room. Gina handed Andrea the defib patches.

"Shock him at one hundred and twenty joules," Noah said.

Andrea's heart lodged in her throat as she placed the patches on her patient's chest, attached the cable, and charged the defibrillator. They had biphasic defibrillators, which enabled them to shock patients at a lower joule level. "All clear?"

Everyone stepped back with their hands lifted to indicate they weren't touching the bed.

"Shocking at one twenty." Andrea delivered the shock. It took a moment for the monitor to capture the heart rhythm. "Still V-fib."

"Shock again at two hundred," Noah commanded.

"All clear? Shocking at two hundred." Andrea glanced at the people around the bed, then delivered the second shock. *Come on*, she thought, watching Mr. Braun's heart rate. Convert already. "Still V-fib."

"Shock him again at two hundred," Noah said.

They repeated the procedure two more times, before Mr. Braun's heart rate converted from the life-threatening heart rhythm to a normal pattern. "Sinus rhythm rate of ninety-eight beats per minute." She eyed Noah. "Let's check for a pulse."

"I feel a carotid pulse." Noah's dark-brown eyes were locked on hers. "Good work. I'll get the cardiology team up here. I'm not sure this is all related to his post-operative pneumonia."

"Sounds good." She managed a smile, doing her best to ignore the weird attraction she felt around Noah. Totally inappropriate considering the seriousness of the situation. And even more so because she had no interest in getting involved in a relationship.

She took another set of vital signs and quickly documented the mini resuscitation in the patient's medical record. She could admire Noah Weston for being a good doctor. That didn't mean she needed to start fantasizing about the man.

From the moment she'd become a nurse, she'd avoided dating any of the doctors she'd met while on duty. Nothing against them personally, but over time, she'd noticed some, not all, ended up cheating on their spouses and girlfriends. Working closely together for long hours in an emotionally charged atmosphere tended to create a closeness that could easily turn into something more than simple camaraderie.

Eight years ago, Andrea had married Stuart, who'd seemed like the perfect guy. Sweet, kind, and funny. He didn't work in the medical field; he'd worked in sales. They'd had two beautiful children, and Stuart had been a good father, at least when he was around. She'd thought their marriage was solid until he'd died while on a road trip in Kentucky, a few miles outside of Lexington. He'd been hit by a semitruck and was killed instantly in the crash.

The worst part was that her husband hadn't been alone in the car. He'd had his mistress with him. A woman named Charlene Temple. Charlie for short. It was only after Stuart's death that she'd realized the Charlie he'd often spoken about as a good friend was really a woman. Not someone who he was simply friends with.

A beautiful woman ten years her junior that he'd been sleeping with while being out on his so-called sales trips for almost two years.

Two years. Andrea still couldn't believe how clueless she'd been. Yet really, how was she supposed to know Stuart was cheating? He'd never gotten impatient with her or the kids. Things were good between them as far as she'd been able to tell. He'd even gotten along well with her parents and five siblings.

After Stuart's death, she'd been forced to admit that she hadn't really known the man she'd married. It was as if Stuart had a split personality. Never in her wildest imagination had she considered he'd cheat on her. His parents, like hers, had been together for years. That Stuart could smile and claim to love her at the same time he was seeing someone else was incomprehensible.

Worst of all, she had learned that not only had he been sleeping with Charlie, but according to some of the text messages and emails that had been uncovered after his death, he'd also been planning to file for divorce.

Leaving her and the kids for his young mistress.

NOAH WESTON KEPT one eye on Andrea and their patient as he discussed Kevin Braun's case with the cardiology fellow, agreeing they should get a cardiac catheterization to look at his coronary arteries. Andrea Monroe was one of the more seasoned nurses in the ICU, and he had come to appreciate her instincts when it came to patient care.

She was beautiful and smart, and a widow with two kids. Yet according to the ICU rumor mill, she had a policy against dating doctors on staff. Her choice. Obviously, she could see anyone she wanted, but he'd often wondered why she had such an ironclad rule. Was it just that she didn't want to get involved with someone at work? Breakups could be messy, as he had seen firsthand among his colleagues. Or was there more to the story?

He'd been intrigued by Andrea, as he was also a widower. He'd lost his wife, a former nurse, to cancer two years ago. Losing her had been difficult, but over time, his grief had faded to the point he'd started looking at other women with interest. Was it wrong to want to find the same type of love he'd experienced with Josie? His pastor had been supportive of Noah getting out there to meet people.

There was no rush, though. Especially since he had his critical care fellowship to get through first.

"Dr. Weston? Call for you on line three." The unit clerk's voice dragged him from his thoughts.

"Thanks." He stepped to the closest phone. "Weston."

"We have a multiple trauma coming in via the Lifeline chopper as a direct admission to the SICU." The caller was his resident, Sean Pollard. "I'm heading up to the helipad to meet the flight team now. They just made it through the worsening storm. The crew will be grounded after this transfer."

He sighed. Why was he the last to know these things? He turned to eye the electronic census board. "What's the name?"

"Jason Dobbs, he's a twenty-five-year-old with multiple fractures, a ruptured spleen, and a head injury."

Not good. "Okay, we'll be waiting." He lowered the phone and walked to the unit clerk's desk. "Did you know about a new trauma case?"

"Oh, yeah." The woman flushed. "Sorry, I was going to tell you about that. I don't think he'll be here soon, though, with the storm."

He arched a brow. "The Lifeline chopper just landed. He's here. Which room can we use?"

The unit clerk's eyes widened in alarm. "Really? I just assumed . . ." She swallowed hard, then said, "I need to tell Andrea, she's the charge nurse. I'll put him in room ten. That's next to Andrea's other patient."

"I'll tell her." He turned and strode down the hallway. "Andrea? New trauma case coming down from the helipad to bed ten."

She grimaced but didn't bother to complain. "Okay, I'll be there in a moment." She finished up with Mr. Braun, then hurried over. "I can't believe the chopper made it through the snowstorm."

"They won't be heading out again anytime soon." He tucked his hands into the pockets of his lab coat. "Sorry about the short notice."

She shrugged, focusing on checking supplies. Then she used her ID badge to log into the computer. "Jason Dobbs?"

"That's the one." He smiled. "Hopefully, Mr. Braun will be heading down for his cardiac catheterization soon. That should free up some of your time."

"They said twenty minutes." She arched a brow. "Nice of you to be concerned about my workload, but I'll manage."

"I know you will." He'd come to appreciate her calm demeanor during a crisis. "Nothing gets you too riled up."

She frowned and gestured to the snow falling outside. "I don't know, you might see me get riled up if I can't get home after my shift. It's Christmas Eve, and I really want to be home with my kids. I mean, they love their grandparents, aunts, and uncles, but I want to be there when they open their gifts tomorrow morning."

He nodded in understanding. "Of course you do. You'll be able to leave as long as they don't declare a snow emergency." That was a possibility his attending Dr. John Crowley had warned him about. Noah hadn't been too concerned. It wasn't as if he had a reason to rush home on the holiday.

But he could empathize with Andrea. Not seeing your own kids on Christmas Eve would be tough. He hoped, for her sake, it wouldn't come to that.

Before Andrea could respond, a heart monitor began to alarm. She spun away, going out into the hallway. He followed her, expecting the alarm to be coming from Mr. Braun's room, but it was the new patient being wheeled in from the helipad accompanied by his resident.

"We need blood transfusions, stat!" Sean Pollard looked distraught. "His blood pressure is tanking, big time."

"Four units of O-negative, we don't have time to do a

cross-match," he told Andrea. "We may need the rapid infuser."

"Got it." Andrea placed her earpiece in and used the portable phone she wore around her neck to get the blood. Then she glanced at a tech. "Get the rapid infuser from the storeroom."

The tech nodded and ran to do her bidding. Andrea joined him in the room, quickly getting their patient connected to the heart monitor.

"What do you think is the source of his bleeding?" Noah asked Sean. Without waiting, he lifted the patient's gown to examine his belly.

"The ruptured spleen, maybe his liver," Sean replied.

The tight abdomen had him nodding in agreement. "We're going to need to do an exploratory lap as soon as we get his pressure stabilized."

Andrea had connected their patient to the monitor and was double-checking the IVs. "Would you like his fluids wide open until the blood gets here?"

"Yes." He would have expected they'd already be running wide open. He eyed the monitor. Pulse was tachy, respirations were steady on the ventilator, but Jason's blood pressure was still too low. "How long for the blood to get here?"

"A minute or two at the most." Andrea didn't look at him as she worked with the IV lines. "They'll send them through the pneumatic tube system."

The hospital he'd previously worked at didn't have that luxury. Noah had been impressed when he'd seen how quickly items could be sent throughout the hospital.

True to her word, another nurse walked in a moment later carrying all four units of blood. "Four units of O neg?"

"Yes, thanks. Help me double-check them, would you?"

Andrea took two of the units, then looked at the patient's wrist band. She read the information out loud, while the second nurse repeated the data. Seconds later, Andrea had all four units up on the rapid infuser.

"Do you want me to call the OR?" Sean asked, interrupting his thoughts.

Noah eyed the monitor again. "Yeah, get a team ready to go. Andrea, when you have time, we could use another four units of O neg blood to take with us."

"Got it." She worked the lines, double-checked the monitor, then made the call. She worked seamlessly, without seeming to even think about her next action. When that was finished, she used her stethoscope to listen to their patient's heart, lungs, and abdomen. "No bowel sounds." Her expression turned grim. "He's bleeding into his belly."

"I know. We're going down to the OR soon."

"There's no OR suite available," Sean said a moment later.

Not good. "How long until they can open one?"

"Thirty minutes." Sean shrugged. "Maybe sooner. They're closing on an open-heart case, not sure how long it will take to turn the room over for our guy."

Andrea finished her exam, looping her stethoscope around her neck. She didn't address the resident but looked at him. "He may not have thirty minutes."

"I know." He tried to quell the sense of panic. They could continue dumping blood into this kid, but if he was bleeding from a major artery, they'd lose the battle sooner than later.

The best way to save his life was to operate. And soon.

"We have a belly tray in the back room," Andrea said. "If you want to open him here, we'll find a way to make that work."

"Really?" He hadn't done a procedure at the bedside before. Yet as he glanced up at the monitor, he could tell they were running out of time. "Okay, let's do it."

Andra hurried off, returning with the necessary supplies. Without wasting a moment, she had the abdominal tray ready and was helping him don a sterile gown, hat, and gloves. Then she called Drake, the respiratory therapist, and asked about what meds he wanted given.

He gave the medication orders, then prepped the patient's belly with antiseptic. Noah had done this procedure many times in his six years of surgical residency, but never in the ICU without a full OR team supporting him.

As he was about to start the time-out, the overhead lights flickered, then shut off. He froze, as it took a moment for the generator to kick on, bringing the lights back on.

He caught Andrea's worried gaze. Then she flashed a reassuring smile. "We're good."

"We're here to do an exploratory laparotomy on patient Jason Dobbs to assess for uncontrolled bleeding into his abdominal cavity."

"Pain meds are on board," Andrea announced. "Suction is ready to go."

He nodded and took the scalpel off the tray. As he made the small incision, using gauze and the suction to remove the blood, he heard a long beep come over the hospital intercom system.

"All hospital staff be advised we are issuing a snow emergency effective immediately. I repeat, all staff be advised we are issuing a snow emergency. No staff are allowed to leave the hospital without permission. We promise to update you soon with further information. Thank you."

There was a long pause as a strange silence fell over the

unit as the staff absorbed the news. He could tell that while they'd suspected this could happen, hearing the declaration hit hard. Yet there was nothing else to do except go back to work. He eyed Andrea, who supported their patient as he continued to operate.

As if she just hadn't been told they'd be working through Christmas until the blizzard was over.

2

———————

Andrea forced herself to stay focused on her patient, despite the declaration of a snow emergency. She couldn't bear the thought of missing the holiday with her children, but that was something to think about later. Right now, Noah was working hard to keep this young man alive, and she needed to do her part too.

Gina brought another four units of blood into the room. "Thanks. Let's check this in, okay?"

"Of course." Gina went through the two-person verification process to ensure they were giving the correct blood to the correct patient. When they were finished, Andrea hung the next two units of blood. They would be used the moment the previous two units were infused.

"Gina, will you keep an eye on Mr. Braun?" Andrea glanced at her. "We're waiting for cardiology to take him to the cath lab."

"Yes. I think I saw the cardiology fellow in his room. I'll let you know when he goes down." Gina quickly left.

Andrea appreciated the way her nursing colleagues

chipped in to help during a crisis. As the charge nurse, she wasn't supposed to have a full patient assignment. Yet that rule didn't mean much when patients continued to roll in.

"I need more suction," Noah said.

She hurried over to change out the suction canister that had filled with their young patient's blood. "Should be okay now," she said.

Noah nodded without looking at her. His resident, Sean, was assisting Noah with the procedure. She eyed the monitor, somewhat relieved to note Jason's blood pressure was stable. Still low, but the blood transfusions she was giving were working to keep him from completely bottoming out.

"I found the bleeder," Noah announced. "Hand me a suture."

Sean did so while continuing to suction blood from Jason's abdominal cavity. She hoped that meant the bleeding would slow down. She alternated between watching the blood transfusions, Jason's vitals, and the suction canister that was already half full.

"It's not pretty, but it should hold until we can get him to the OR," Noah said a few minutes later. "Andrea, I need dressings to pack the wound."

"Coming up." She darted to the supply cart and removed several large abdominal dressings. She quickly opened them up one by one on the sterile field. Noah flashed a grateful smile as he began to pack them into the wound, counting out loud.

"Six dressings," he announced. "Andrea, can you make a note of that in the record?"

"Yes." She took a moment to slow the blood transfusions, as Jason's blood pressure had begun to recover. Then she logged onto the computer to make the notation. She knew that counting dressings was important as the last thing they wanted was to accidentally leave one buried inside a patient. A retained foreign object was a big lawsuit waiting to happen.

Her phone rang. She placed the earpiece in to answer. "This is Andrea."

"This is Amy from the OR. We're ready for Jason Dobbs in OR suite ten."

"Great. We'll bring him right down." She disconnected from the line. "Room ten in the OR is available."

"Great." Noah looked as relieved as she felt, knowing Jason would soon be getting the care he needed. Noah had done a good job of stabilizing him, though. She was humbled by how quickly Noah had jumped to do what was necessary to save this young man's life.

"I'll grab the portable monitor." Andrea headed out to the supply room. Moments later, she had Jason disconnected from the bedside monitor and ready to roll.

Accompanied by Drake the respiratory therapist, Noah, and Sean, they headed out of the ICU to the elevator. Andrea kept a wary eye on the monitor; the last thing she wanted was to code a patient in the elevator. Thankfully, Jason was stable for the ride down to the operating rooms. A trauma surgeon by the name of Wyatt Cramer and an anesthesiologist, Jack Kline, waited for them in OR 10.

As she helped get Jason connected to the OR equipment with Jack Kline, she listened as Noah described what he'd found and the temporary suturing he'd performed at the bedside.

"Sounds good," Wyatt said with a nod. "We'll get him squared away from here."

"We packed six abdominal dressings in the wound," Andrea added. "You'll want to be sure you get that many back out again."

"Understood," Wyatt agreed. "Nice work, Noah."

With the transfer complete, she and Drake wheeled the empty bed out into the hallway. It would need to be cleaned before bringing it back up to the surgical ICU.

Leaving the bed behind, Andrea picked up the portable monitor. It wasn't heavy as much as it was bulky.

"I'll take that." Noah grabbed the monitor from her arms. "I kinda wish I could stay down here to finish the procedure I started."

She nodded, walking beside him back to the elevators. She could appreciate his wanting to have follow through. "I get it. But we have a full unit of critically ill patients upstairs."

"I know." Noah flashed a grin. "Gotta say, critical care is never boring."

She managed to smile back at him. "Never. That's why we like it so much."

Truly, she did enjoy her job. But as they returned to the ICU, Andrea thought again about the fact that the hospital administrators had declared a snow emergency. She needed to call her parents to let them know she'd be delayed indefinitely.

She washed her hands, then headed to Mr. Braun's room. It was empty. As she turned away, she saw Gina walking toward her.

"Hey," Gina said. "Mr. Braun is down in the cath lab."

"Good to know." Andrea glanced at her watch. It was five in the evening. "I need to make a quick call. Then I'll round on the unit to help out."

"No problem." Gina turned and headed toward her patient's room.

Andrea ducked into the staff break room. There was nobody back there, so she pulled out her cell phone and called home. Her brother Alec answered. He was the only non-medical sibling in the family, but he'd married Jillian, who was now a neurology physician. "Hi, Andrea."

"How are Bethany and Ben doing?" Her gaze lingered on the scrawny Christmas tree they'd put up right after Thanksgiving. It was decorated with streams of gauze as garland and small square dressings cut into snowflake shapes. Using hospital supplies was probably against the rules, but nobody seemed to mind. Right now, she couldn't help but think about the beautiful tree in her parents' living room and wished she were heading home sooner rather than later.

"They're fine. We're getting ready to eat dinner shortly," Alec said. "Do you want us to save a plate for you?"

"No, that's why I'm calling. The hospital declared a snow emergency." She eyed the snow piling up outside the window, a thick blanket of white. She hoped that everyone who'd wanted a white Christmas was happy, because she certainly wasn't. "I'll have to stay until they declare the emergency over."

"Oh man, sorry to hear that, sis," Alec said with sympathy. "According to the news, they don't anticipate the snow stopping until tomorrow morning."

She closed her eyes against the prick of tears. If that were true, then she'd be stuck there until later in the morning, well after the time her kids opened their presents. She drew in a deep breath and tried not to sound as miserable as she felt. "Will you let the kids know I'll be there as soon as I can?"

"Of course, don't worry. Bethany and Ben are having a great time with their cousins."

She knew her brother was right, but that didn't make the

ache in her chest feel any better. "Okay, thanks, Alec. I'll call later to talk to the kids before they go to sleep."

"Sounds good. Meanwhile, we'll all pray the snow stops soon," Alec said. "Later, Andrea."

"Bye." She lowered the phone, blinked back her tears, and sniffled. This wasn't the worst thing in the world. Her kids would be fine. Swiping at her face, she jumped up, turned, and almost ran smack into Noah.

He caught her shoulders with his hands. "Hey, are you okay?" His intense brown eyes were full of concern. No doubt he'd noticed her crying.

The urge to step closer was strong, and it took all of Andrea's willpower to resist the temptation. Her rule about keeping doctors at arm's length suddenly seemed foolish. Shaking that thought off, she reminded herself that she was a single mother with two kids. There was no time for a personal life. "I'm fine." She pasted a smile on her face. "Just called home to let them know I'm working late."

"I'm sure it's not easy for you to be away from your kids at Christmas," Noah murmured. He still held her shoulders in his skilled hands.

"They're with their cousins." She grimaced and added, "They won't miss me as much as I'll miss them."

Noah's expression was full of compassion. "They love you, Andrea. And I'm sure once this snow emergency is over, they'll be thrilled to see you."

"You're right." She told herself to stop being foolish. Her kids were happy and healthy. There were worse things than working through Christmas.

"I'm sure part of this is that you're missing your husband." His gaze was solemn. "I know it's not easy to get through the holidays after losing a spouse."

She remembered hearing Noah was a widower too. She knew she should agree with him, there was no need to let him or anyone else know the truth about Stuart, but somehow, she found herself saying, "Considering my husband was cheating on me when he was in that fatal car crash, I don't miss him."

Noah's eyes widened with horror. "I'm sorry. I didn't know."

"Nobody knows here at the hospital. Only my family." It was a secret she'd carried alone for the past eighteen months, and she had no idea why she'd blurted it out now. "Just forget I said anything. Excuse me." She slipped out of Noah's grasp and headed back out to the unit. There were patients to care for.

Keeping busy was the best way to forget about her personal issues.

SHOCKED BY HER REVELATION, Noah stared after Andrea as she left the break room. He couldn't believe her husband had been cheating on her when he'd died. Andrea was not only beautiful, skilled, and smart, but she had two kids. How her husband could throw his family away like garbage, he had no idea.

He wondered if Andrea's husband had been a physician or a fellow nurse. Was that the reason she had a no-dating-doctors rule? Why did he care anyway? Giving himself a mental shake, he crossed over to the coffeepot. Grimacing at the thick sludge inside, he proceeded to make a fresh pot. If they were going to be stuck here all night, then they'd need plenty of caffeine to get through the next twelve to fourteen hours.

Normally, his rotation would be over at seven thirty in

the evening, the same shift change as the nurses. But glancing at the thick blanket of snow outside, he doubted his colleague Jeff Ramos would be there to relieve him. And even if Jeff did show up, being under a snow emergency meant nobody was allowed to leave.

Including the medical staff.

When the coffee finished brewing, he filled his mug, took a sip, then walked out to review the census board. Every room was full, even though Jason and Mr. Braun were off having procedures. One of his responsibilities was to free up a few beds for new emergencies.

For that, he needed to round with Andrea, the charge nurse on duty. He took another sip of his coffee, set the mug in the break room, and headed out to find her.

He found her helping one of the nurses clean up a patient. He waited until they'd finished to ask, "Do you have time to make rounds?"

"Yes." She washed her hands, then joined him. "I was going to suggest we talk about who we can send out to the floor. If that snow keeps up, we'll see more trauma patients."

"My thoughts exactly." He grabbed a computer mounted on a cart. They called them COWs, computers on wheels. As a joke, the nursing staff had named them. This one was Bessie. They also had Mabel, Clara, and Bertie. "Let's start with room one and make our way around the unit."

Andrea glanced at her watch. "It might be smarter to start with those patients who are not intubated or on IV medications to support their blood pressures. The sick patients aren't going anywhere. There are five patients who are relatively stable. We need to start there."

"Okay, tell me who you think is the best out of those five to transfer out." He would need to make rounds on the other patients eventually, but for now, he'd prioritize those who could be bumped out to the general floor.

"Ms. Landcaster is post-op day one from her open-heart surgery." Andrea gestured to the heart monitor over her head. "Her vitals have been stable. The surgeon wanted to keep her here until morning, but if push comes to shove, she can go."

Noah took a moment to review the woman's medical record. After a moment, he nodded in agreement. Dr. Finegold would not be happy about her being bumped, but he had to admit Andrea was right. She was stable, and even now, the nurse had her sitting up on the edge of the bed eating a few ice chips. "Okay, I'll write orders for her to be sent to the floor. What else do we have?"

Andrea moved onto the next patient. Fifteen minutes later, he had orders written for two patients to be transferred out, Mrs. Landcaster and another post-operative trauma patient who'd suffered a chest injury.

Feeling better about having a couple of empty beds, he returned to the break room to finish his coffee. He watched the storm, thinking of Andrea's kids getting ready for Christmas. He and Josie had wanted kids, but once she was diagnosed with an aggressive form of brain cancer, that hadn't happened.

Was it easier for Andrea to get over her husband's death having the kids to distract her? Maybe. Then again, she'd had to deal with her husband's betrayal on top of his demise.

A triple beeping alarm pulled him from his thoughts. He set his empty cup aside and strode out into the unit. Triple beeping generally indicated an emergency, and sure enough, several staff members, including Andrea, ran into a room.

He quickly joined them. He knew the patient, Tomas Nelson, was another elderly patient who'd been in a car crash two days ago. At eighty-one, the older man had suffered broken ribs and a broken pelvis along with a liver laceration. He'd been one of the five patients who wasn't on a ventilator, but Noah had been concerned about the older man's heart.

"Sats dropped to eighty, pulse is tachy at one ten." Andrea glanced at him. "He may need to be intubated."

Noah didn't like the idea. At his age, getting him off the ventilator wouldn't be easy. But when he'd tried to discuss code status with the patient earlier that morning, the guy had insisted he wanted everything done. Swallowing a wave of frustration, he nodded. "I'll get the intubation cart."

He'd barely taken two steps when Andrea called, "Noah? I don't feel a pulse. He's in PEA."

Pulseless electrical activity was a life-threatening rhythm. He turned back to the room. The only treatment for PEA, other than performing CPR, was to rectify the underlining cause.

"Let's use a bougie airway," he said. That was something the respiratory therapist could do as it was less invasive than inserting an ETT. "I need stat labs, gasses, full chemistry panel, and cardiac enzymes, including a troponin."

Andrea was performing CPR. Another staff member drew blood from the patient's arterial line.

Once the patient's oxygen levels improved, he moved over to check for a pulse. Then he said, "Stop CPR."

Andrea stopped. Instantly, the pulse beneath his fingertips vanished. The patient's heart appeared to be working, but wasn't.

Not good. "Continue CPR."

Andrea went back to work. From the pained expression

on her face, he knew she'd broken a few ribs, a common complication of CPR, especially in elderly patients. This was why he preferred not to have patients Tom's age as a full code.

But there was nothing he could do now except keep going. As he continued filtering through different diagnoses related to the underlying cause of this cardiac arrest, he was struck by the stark contrast between the way Josie had died peacefully in his arms and the full-out CPR they were doing now.

This wasn't what he'd want for his loved one at this patient's age, but his wishes didn't matter.

"Labs are back, he's severely acidotic," Gina said. "Maybe septic?"

He nodded, that was one of the many thoughts he'd had. "We can try antibiotics. Hold CPR."

Andrea halted, breathing hard. After still feeling no pulse, he sighed. "Continue CPR, but, Andrea, you should take a break."

"I'll take over." Gina nudged her colleague aside and began providing compressions.

"Do you want me to start antibiotics?" Andrea asked.

"I'll order broad spectrum antibiotics." It felt like a futile task, as they didn't know the source of his infection, but it was likely his lungs. Still, it was the next step in the process, so he went ahead and ordered them anyway. Andrea went to the automated dispensing machine and removed the medication. As she hung the minibag, he eyed the clock. "We'll continue CPR until this dose is in. If that doesn't change anything, I'm calling it."

Andrea nodded in understanding. By her expression, he knew she shared his concern. There was little they could do to change this patient's outcome, but as a physician, he was bound by ethics to give it his best try.

They continued the resuscitation for another twenty minutes. When Noah was satisfied that he'd done everything possible, he called it. "Stop CPR." No surprise, there was still no pulse beneath his fingers. "Okay, I'm calling this over. Time of death is 1802."

There was a moment of silence as they stepped back from the bedside. Losing a patient was never easy, but in this case, Noah sensed they were all relieved he'd ended the resuscitation.

He turned away, drawing Bessie to the side so he could document the event. Despite doing everything according to Advanced Life Support protocol, he felt as if he'd failed his patient.

Maybe if he'd spent more time with Tomas, he'd have been able to convince the man to accept a peaceful death with dignity. In his experience, it was harder for those without faith in God to accept death. And this was one of those cases. The old man had stubbornly insisted he wanted everything done, so Noah tried to take heart that he'd followed their patient's wishes.

"Noah? Are you okay?" Andrea's low voice had him glancing at her.

"Yeah." He ruefully shook his head. "I feel bad we had to put him through that."

"I know. I hate when I feel ribs cracking while doing CPR." She glanced over to where Tomas Nelson lay still. "If patients knew what 'doing everything' meant, they'd never agree to being resuscitated."

"I explained it to him in great detail." Noah finished his note and logged off the computer. "He was too afraid of dying."

She nodded. "I've seen that a lot. Our family was raised with faith, but back when my father suffered a heart attack, it wasn't easy to accept the possibility of losing him."

"My wife died peacefully in my arms." He flushed when she turned to stare at him. "She was ready to be out of pain, and while I knew she was up in heaven with Jesus, it was still the hardest thing I've ever done."

"I can only imagine." Andrea rested her hand on his arm. "You're a good man, Noah. A wonderful husband and an amazing doctor. We're lucky to have you."

Her sweet praise warmed his heart. The attraction he'd experienced since the first time they'd met sizzled in the air between them. As she stared up at him with her green eyes, he wondered if she felt it too. For a long moment, it was as if they were alone. Everything around them had faded away.

Then the unit clerk's voice rang out. "Andrea? You have a call on line one. Sounds like your patient from the cath lab is ready to return."

"Excuse me." Andrea dropped her hand and turned to reach for the closest phone. He listened to her side of the conversation for a moment, then turned back to look at the census board.

He shoved his hands into the pockets of his lab coat. They were in the middle of a snow emergency, surrounded by critically ill patients. This was not the time or the place to be thinking about how much he wanted to see Andrea outside of the hospital setting. For the first time since Josie's passing, he didn't feel guilty for wanting to spend time with another woman.

Yet even if he did summon the courage to ask her out, he already knew she'd refuse. Unless she'd somehow changed her mind about her rule? Yeah, probably not.

With a heavy sigh, he pushed Bessie down the hall.
Time to get back to work.

3

———

Andrea tried her best to ignore the acute awareness she felt for Noah as she examined Mr. Braun's post-cardiac catheterization. His groin site was dry and intact, which was good. The cardiology attending informed her they'd placed three stints in her patient's coronary arteries. If he'd needed more than that, they'd have taken him to the operating room for bypass surgery. Looking up at the monitor, she was grateful to see his vitals were stable. After losing their elderly patient, it was nice to have a success story.

Working critical care could be emotionally draining. Yet she loved her job, most of the time. Bad days aside, they generally cared for the sickest patients, treating and stabilizing them until they'd recovered enough to be transferred out. Sometimes their patients came back to thank them. That was the greatest reward of all.

"How long do I have to remain flat?" Mr. Braun asked in a raspy voice. They'd removed the breathing tube post catheterization, and she wondered if he realized how close he'd come to dying today.

"Eight hours." She patted his arm. "Try to get some rest."

He grimaced but nodded and closed his eyes.

Glancing at her watch, she sighed when she realized it was a quarter past seven in the evening. Normally, the next shift of nurses would be in, ready to relieve them. After documenting her note on Mr. Braun, she headed into the break room. The only person in there was Gretta, and from the resigned expression in her colleague's eyes, she knew there was no relief coming.

"Nobody from the night shift has come in?" Andrea had expected at least one or two nurses to have made it through the storm.

Gretta shook her head. "I figure we'll all keep our same patient assignments."

"Yeah." Outside, thick snowflakes continued to fall. The last report she'd seen indicated they'd gotten six inches of snow in the past three hours, with more to come. Andrea hated to admit the snow was pretty. She could imagine her kids building snowmen and making snow forts in the morning. Maybe she'd be home in time to help them. Swallowing a pang of regret, she said, "I'll keep Mr. Braun and take the first admission."

"No, I'm up for the first admit. You're not supposed to have a patient assignment." Gretta sipped her coffee. "I transferred Mary Landcaster to the floor. And there are two other nurses with only one patient. We've agreed we'll take the new admissions before you do." Gretta set her empty cup aside. "Time to get back to work."

Andrea poured herself some coffee, knowing she was going to need it. Twelve-hour shifts were long enough without adding an all-nighter to the mix. Glumly, she stared at the snow as she downed some badly needed caffeine. She knew she was making a bigger deal out of this snow emergency than she should be, but she couldn't help it. As a single mother, missing Christmas morning was inconceivable. Yet there was no point in brooding.

They couldn't leave. They were all stuck here until morning.

Thinking about how Noah had held his wife as she passed away brought a wave of guilt. Missing the holiday was nothing compared to what some people were dealing with. Time to stop feeling sorry for herself.

Would Stuart have held her in his arms the same way? She honestly couldn't imagine him doing that. He always claimed he had a weak stomach and left all the first aid and other caregiver types of tasks to her.

Whatever. It didn't matter now. Stuart was gone, and she was better off without him. Maybe if Stuart hadn't been cheating, if he'd been more like Noah . . . but he wasn't.

Enough. Nothing good came from making comparisons. Sipping more coffee, she stared at her reflection in the window. She needed to get over this crush she had on Noah Weston. She didn't date doctors. Even handsome and seemingly sweet guys like him.

As the thought formed, though, she was forced to acknowledge it was a stupid rule. Stuart wasn't a doctor and had still cheated. And she knew there were several physicians on staff who were dedicated to their spouses. Their medical director of the SICU, Dr. John Wainright, had been married to his wife for thirty-five years.

And she knew Noah would have been married to his wife for the rest of their lives if that had been possible. She was wise enough now to recognize the signs of those who were easily led astray by their hormones. When she'd been a new graduate nurse, she'd been swayed by a handsome resident who'd lavished her with praise and attention. Only to find out after he'd kissed her that he was married.

Horrified, she'd decided then and there she'd never date another doctor again. But the failure wasn't hers, it was Tyler Brigg's. That cheating resident was a big-wig thoracic surgeon on staff here at Trinity Medical Center now, and he was on his third wife. Why he kept getting married, she had no idea. If he wanted to cheat, he should have just stayed single.

Turning away, she set her coffee aside and headed out into the unit. It was time to make rounds. Spotting Noah down by bed 1, she hurried over to join him.

"Hey." He smiled warmly.

Flustered, she glanced at the patient lying in the bed. "Let's round on these patients before we get slammed with another admission."

"Works for me," he agreed.

For the next thirty minutes, they covered the sixteen patients who remained. Three empty beds, soon to be four when the deceased patient was sent to the morgue and the room cleaned, would likely be filled by morning.

Unless everyone in the city was smart enough to stay home during a blizzard.

Which wasn't likely.

"What do you think about bumping Mr. Braun to the general floor if we need a bed?" Noah's question interrupted her thoughts.

"He's stable enough post cath, but he did arrest earlier." She shrugged. "We'll see how he looks in a few hours."

"Sounds good, but I'm going to put him at the top of the bump list." Noah made a note in the computer. "Mr. Decker concerns me. He's still very septic, not responding well to vasopressors and antibiotics."

"I know." Mr. Decker had suffered a traumatic gut injury, several stab wounds to the belly during some gang war. "His delay in coming in for treatment really put us at a disadvantage."

Noah held her gaze, and she knew he was thinking the same thing she was. Knife wounds along with gunshot wounds were an automatic report to the police. Their patient Marcus Decker hadn't wanted the police called because he had a criminal record. By the time one of his buddies had dropped him off in the emergency department, he was in full-blown septic shock.

"We're doing our best." She managed a reassuring smile. Noah seemed to take any failure in saving a patient personally, even though they both knew the best medical care in the world couldn't save them all. "He's young. Hopefully, he'll pull through this."

"Yeah." His expression remained grim. "How are you? Doing okay?"

"Me?" She tried not to blush at his concern. "I'm fine."

"None of this is easy." Noah raked his hand through his thick dark hair. "We're in for a long night."

Before she could respond, the doors to the ICU opened and two hospital administrators walked in pushing a cart laden with wrapped sandwiches and soft drinks. Andrea was surprised and gestured for them to bring the cart into the break room.

"We're making rounds on all the units, bringing dinner for everyone." Trish Patterson, the vice president of nursing, smiled. "This is our way of thanking you for being understanding of the snow emergency."

"Thanks, the staff will be thrilled to have dinner." It wasn't the Christmas meal her mother would have made, but Andrea was touched by the gesture. And she was also surprised Trish had stayed. Her boss, Debra Crow, had left early to beat the storm. Andrea had assumed most of the hospital administrators had done the same.

Noah came into the room, looking surprised at the cart full of food. "Any idea how long the snow emergency will last?"

"We're hearing the snow might end about two or three in the morning," Ron Hobert said. He was the house supervisor for the off shifts, which included holidays. "But we'll need to be sure there's enough time for the roads to be cleared before we can expect the staff to make their way in."

That sounded reasonable. Andrea touched the portable phone around her neck and made an all call to her peers. "Dinner in the break room."

"We'd better move on to the next unit," Trish said. "Thanks again and Merry Christmas."

The administrators left as staff nurses trickled into the break room to grab a sandwich. Andrea ate one, too, but noticed Noah hung back, not taking anything for himself until everyone else had gotten something to eat. His residents had helped themselves.

She was impressed by his chivalry.

As she headed back to check on Mr. Braun, she couldn't help but acknowledge Noah was everything she would have wanted in a husband.

Too bad she wasn't in the market for a relationship.

AFTER HAULING Bessie into the break room, Noah sat in front of the computer, munched on his sandwich, and reviewed Marcus Decker's chart. The kid's vitals were hanging on by a thread, and if they didn't rebound soon, he was certain they'd be resuscitating him next.

They were doing everything medically possible to save him. What bothered him the most was that this kid would have already been out of the hospital and home recovering if he hadn't delayed getting treatment.

Yet he knew there had to be rules to report specific injuries to law enforcement. Marcus probably underestimated the severity of his injury. A tough lesson to learn that being arrested wasn't nearly as bad as dying of septic shock.

There was another patient, Albert Holland, who was also extremely ill. He'd had open-heart surgery three days ago, but he'd suffered bleeding that had required two more trips to the OR. His condition was relatively stable for the moment, but the multiple surgeries had set him back. He was also maxed out on vasopressors to maintain his blood pressure and ventilator settings to support his lungs.

Andrea came into the room, her phone in hand. Seeing him, she flushed. "Hey. Just calling home to check on the kids."

"No problem." He stood and tossed the sandwich wrapping into the garbage. "I'll give you some privacy."

"No need, it's fine." She turned and lifted her phone to her ear. "Hi, Mom, how are the kids?"

Noah heard the slight hitch in her voice. He left the break room, feeling bad for what she was going through. He was sure other staff members were also missing family time at Christmas; she wasn't the only one. Yet Andrea being a widowed single mother touched his heart.

The good news was that she had family to support her kids in her absence.

His pager went off. Swallowing a groan, he looked at the message. No surprise they were getting a new trauma patient in. A twenty-eight-year-old male, Roger Greenwald, had suffered bilateral leg fractures and a traumatic brain injury after being involved in a motor-vehicle crash.

He glanced back at Andrea who was still on the phone, then walked over to the electronic census board. The unit clerk had a half-eaten sandwich at her desk. When she looked up at him, he held up the pager. "New admit is on the way."

"That figures." She sighed loudly and reached for the phone. "I'll ask Andrea which room she wants me to use."

"No need, I'll ask her." Noah figured that would give Andrea a few extra minutes to talk to her kids. "Do you know who's up for the first admit?"

"Gretta, she's in room five." The clerk glanced at the census board. "We may as well use bed seven; it's close to her current patient."

"Why don't you do that. I'll clear it with Andrea. Please call the respiratory therapist too. This guy is a multiple trauma with a head injury. He may need to be intubated." He turned away, already thinking about the new patient. He wondered what had caused the car crash. Surprising anyone had tried to get out in this storm.

Andrea walked out of the break room, her gaze down on her phone. She almost ran into him but stopped abruptly. "Sorry."

"No worries." She hadn't been crying, so he took that as a positive sign. "We have a multiple trauma coming up from the ED in a few minutes. I heard Gretta is up next, and we thought putting the patient in room seven was for the best."

"That works. Who on earth was out in this weather?" She shook her head in amazement. "At least the snow should be enough to keep the gang activity to a minimum."

"I should hope so." He knew some of the staff joked

about the knife-and-gun club coming out to play. The sad truth was that they had a gunshot or knife wound coming into the emergency department almost every other day. The weekends were usually the worst. Even holidays like Christmas and New Year's Eve didn't necessarily bring the crime rate down.

A blizzard was different, though, so that was one point in their favor. Even the most die-hard criminal tended to stay inside.

Andrea hurried over to chat with Gretta. He quickly checked on the two sickest patients in the unit before he heard the telltale beat of a portable monitor as the double doors opened and their patient was wheeled through.

Noah strode down to bed 7, where Andrea and Gretta flanked the new patient. The ED doc was giving them the lowdown.

"Twenty-eight-year-old Cole Slatter was in a crash that involved his pickup truck being struck by a city snowplow," the resident said. "Pretty much crushed him head-on. Airbags deployed, but he's been very confused and combative. Small intracranial bleed via CT scan, but you'll need to keep an eye on him. We dosed him with ten milligrams of Versed, and he's still awake and moving." As if to prove the resident's point, the young man thrashed his head from side to side and thumped his restrained hand on the bed.

"Impressive," Gretta drawled. "He's a big guy."

Cole Slater was solid muscle and looked like he could be an offensive lineman for the Green Bay Packers. Ten milligrams was probably light for his weight. Considering he had a breathing tube in place and was on a ventilator to assist with his breathing, Noah felt there was no reason to be too cautious with the drugs. "Get another ten milligrams of Versed ready. We'll need it to perform a thorough exam."

"On it," Andrea said, leaving the room.

When Gretta moved to untie one of the kid's arms, Noah stopped her. "Let's wait until the medication has been given."

"Okay." Gretta began to stick EKG patches on his chest. "No chest hair, Cole must be a professional body builder."

"Or a serial killer," Andrea joked as she reentered the room. At his shocked expression, she shrugged. "Just kidding. Although some serial killers do shave their body to avoid leaving forensic evidence behind."

He couldn't help smiling at that. "Let's give him the benefit of the doubt on that, shall we?"

"If you say so." Andrea found Cole's IV tubing and traced it back to his arm, then frowned. "This is infiltrated. I'll need to place a new line."

"He has ropes for veins, shouldn't be too difficult," Gretta said as she continued connecting him to the monitor. Cole twisted on the bed, straining against the soft wrist restraints. "Hurry up, though, before any more of the Versed he has on board wears off."

"Working on it." Andrea was doing her best to use sterile technique to place the catheter. No easy task with the way the guy was moving around.

Thankfully, it didn't take too long to thread the catheter into the large veins popping out of Cole's forearm.

"Okay, eighteen gauge IV is in place." Andrea bent to swipe the sweat from her forehead on her scrub sleeve. "Infusing another ten milligrams of Versed now."

"Good." Gretta looked up at the heart monitor. "Pulse of eighty-eight, normal sinus rhythm, and a blood pressure of one twenty-two over fifty. If not for his head injury, I'd ask why they brought him up here."

"His condition could go south, especially if he keeps

fighting us," Andrea said. "I'm concerned his head injury could get worse." She stepped back and disposed of the needle in a sharps container. "We'll give him a few minutes, then untie him to get him repositioned on the bed."

"Okay by me," Gretta agreed. "I hope this second dose does the trick."

"It should," Noah said. "But I'll give another order for more sedation if needed."

Noah entered orders as they watched the patient. When he appeared relaxed, the medication finally kicking in, they began to loosen his restraints.

The moment he was free, the kid's eyes opened, and he immediately went berserk. "No, let me go!" he shouted, and twisted on the bed, lifting his splinted broken legs off the mattress, which had to hurt, and swinging his fists wildly. One closed fist smacked Andrea on the temple, sending her flying backward against the supply cart.

"Stop fighting," Gretta cried, hanging on to his arm with all her strength. "You're in the hospital! Please stop fighting."

The kid was beyond reason. Noah jumped up and rushed forward to grab the man's arm. The patient was strong, and it was all he could do to keep him from breaking free.

"Let me go, let me go," he bellowed loud enough to be heard all the way down in the emergency department. The ED doc should have prepared them better, but the resident was gone now, so it was too late to mention it.

"We need help in here," Gretta called.

Two more staff members rushed in to help. Andrea was slow to get up. He glanced at her but had to focus on their rambunctious patient. It took all four of them to get his wrists tied back down. Andrea pushed herself to her feet, swaying a bit.

"Are you okay?" Satisfied the patient was under control, he turned his attention to her.

With a wince, she held her hand to her temple. "I'll be fine."

He eyed her with concern. The two nurses stepped forward to continue helping Gretta. He guided Andrea away toward the break room. "I want you to sit down."

She didn't respond, which only worried him more. Easing her into a chair, he knelt in front of her. "I might need an ice pack," she whispered.

"I'll get one. Let me see." He lowered her hand from her head. An abrasion marred her ivory skin, and he knew she was right about the ice pack. A dark bruise was already starting to form. "Okay, sit tight. I'll be right back."

Jumping to his feet, he headed out to the main supply room. The cold packs were with the other dressings, and he grabbed one, crushing it between his fingers as he hurried back to Andrea. Kneading the pack, he waited for the chemicals to mix, creating the coldness she needed.

"Here." He knelt beside her and pressed the cold pack to the abrasion. "I'm sorry this happened."

"Yeah, well, who would have thought twenty milligrams of Versed wasn't enough?" She winced. "We should have used an elephant-sized dose."

That made him smile. "Next time."

She closed her eyes for a moment. "Thanks. That feels good."

"I'd like to check your pupils." He reached for the penlight in his breast pocket. "That guy might not be the only one with a head injury."

"I'm fine." She brushed off his concern. "I should have ducked faster."

Ignoring her protest, he flashed the penlight into one

eye and then the other. They were both equal and reactive to light. He sighed in relief and tucked the penlight away. "If anyone is at fault, it's me. I should have gone with a higher dose."

"This isn't the first time I've been hit by a patient." She repositioned the cold pack. "At least he has a head injury to explain his actions. The last patient who slugged me didn't have an excuse."

He shook his head. "Unacceptable."

She managed a wan smile. "Yep."

Logic told him he should move away. There was no reason to hover over her like that. But he couldn't seem to tear his gaze from hers. They were so close, mere inches separating them. Noah dropped his gaze to her mouth. He leaned in to kiss her when a three-beep emergency alarm rang out.

Saved by the bell, he thought as he leaped up and headed out to find the source of the alarm. If he had kissed Andrea, she probably would have smacked him the same way Cole had struck her.

And frankly, he'd have deserved it.

4

———

Her head throbbing painfully, Andrea stood. A wave of dizziness had her pressing her hand to the table to steady herself. Being injured by a patient was no excuse for what she'd nearly done.

Kissing Noah, especially while they were both on duty, was wrong in too many ways to count.

What was she thinking? Clearly, her brains had gotten scrambled by Cole's fist. That was the only explanation for her lack of judgment. Drawing in a deep breath, she set the cold pack aside and forced herself to respond to the emergency alarm.

She was the last to arrive to the scene in Mr. Decker's room. The staff at the bedside, including Noah, were already working on him. Her colleague Sam Davis was doing CPR while Gina pushed medication. This was their fourth resuscitation in the past five hours, and she couldn't help but wonder if that was a new record.

Granted, if not for the snow emergency, she and the rest of the day-shift staff wouldn't be there now. The night-shift crew would have been handling this resuscitation. Regardless, this wasn't a great way to spend Christmas Eve. They'd already lost one patient, she didn't want to think about losing another.

She stood for a moment, then turned away. Since they had this under control, she'd peek in on Sam's and Gina's other patients to make sure they didn't need anything. Plus, she needed to check on Mr. Braun. The time had gotten away from her, thanks to Cole's lethal right hook.

For the next thirty minutes, she did her best to ignore her headache. Mr. Braun was doing well and so were the rest of the patients in the unit. She headed back down toward the ongoing resuscitation, wondering if she had any ibuprofen in her purse.

She didn't think she'd be able to make it all night without some pain relief.

Pausing outside Mr. Decker's room, she was glad to see they'd stopped CPR and that the patient's blood pressure had been restored. His heart rate was still tachy, though.

"Give him another five hundred cc fluid bolus," Noah ordered. "And increase his hourly rate to one fifty cc per hour."

"Got it," Sam said. He quickly hung the fluids. "Are you adding another antibiotic too?"

"Yeah." Noah scowled at the computer screen. "This will be our fourth antibiotic. We're running out of options."

There was a moment of silence as the staff digested that information.

Gina left to grab the medication. Andrea stepped in to help clean up the mess. Things were always chaotic during a resuscitation.

"Thanks, Andrea." Sam frowned when he got a good look at her. "Wow, that bruise looks bad."

"I'm fine." Or she would be once she got some ibuprofen

from her locker. "Do you need help with your other patient?"

"No, thankfully, she's stable."

"Okay, let me know if that changes." Andrea headed back out into the hall. Noah joined her. "Crisis averted," he muttered as they headed back to the break room. "But I don't think he's out of the woods yet."

"I hear you." She avoided his gaze, far too aware of their near kiss. "Excuse me." She ducked through the supply room to enter the staff locker room.

Finding the ibuprofen was a relief. She dumped four tablets into her hand and tossed them back, swallowing them without water. Then she sat on the bench for a minute to close her eyes. The injury could have been worse, but the pain combined with the fatigue of working fifteen hours straight now was wearing on her.

Only nine more hours to go, she thought with a sigh.

"Andrea?" Hearing her name had her eyes popping open in alarm. Noah stood there, hands tucked into his lab coat pockets. "I need to apologize for . . ."

"What? No, you don't." Dear Heaven, she did not want to have this conversation. Her cheeks burned with embarrassment as she jumped up and moved past him. "Everything is fine. I, uh, need to get back to work."

Hunching her shoulders, she braced for him to follow her out of the locker room. When he didn't, she squelched the temptation to look back over her shoulder.

Why on earth would he apologize to her? She was the one who'd almost kissed him. Then it hit her. He was going to apologize for giving her the wrong idea about being interested in anything that remotely resembled a kiss.

She swallowed hard and ducked into Mr. Braun's room. That was even worse, but she knew it was her own fault for allowing herself to be ridiculously touched by Noah's kind consideration of her injury. As if he wouldn't be that nice to any of the other staff members on the unit.

"Can I have some ice chips?" Mr. Braun asked.

"Of course. Turn your head to the side so you don't choke." She spooned a few ice chips into his mouth. "Better?"

"Yeah. But I wish I could sit up." He shifted on the bed. "I called my wife, convinced her to stay home because of the snow."

"That's good." She thought of their new admission, Cole Slatter, being squashed by a snowplow. "It's too dangerous out there."

"I know." He sighed and closed his eyes. "I guess I'll try to get more sleep."

"Call me if you need anything." She stepped over to the computer, documented her assessment of his groin site and his vitals, then logged off. Based on how well he was doing post cath, she had to agree he should be the first one to bump out of the ICU if they needed more open beds.

Hopefully, it wouldn't come to that.

The pounding in her head eased a bit over the next two hours. But when the unit clerk called with a patient needing to transfer back in, her heart sank and the throbbing returned. She found Noah standing outside Mr. Decker's room.

"Noah, Ms. Landcaster has taken a turn for the worse. Dr. Finegold isn't happy we moved her in the first place. He wants her to come back into the ICU."

He grimaced and nodded. "I understand. What's going on?"

"Her blood pressure has dropped, and it sounds like she's throwing some PVCs." Premature ventricular contractions could easily turn into v-tach, a life-threatening arrhythmia. "I told them she could go into room fourteen where she was originally."

"Sounds good. I'll be down to see her shortly." He turned his attention back to Decker's chart. "I wish this kid would turn the corner."

She shared is concern but knew he was doing everything medically possible to save Decker's life. Finding Gina, she discovered the nurse was already on the floor with the floor nurse caring for Ms. Landcaster.

"That's fine. Don't worry about it. Just get her back down here." Gina ended the call. "I feel bad that we sent her out, but now we only have two empty beds."

"It's not your fault. We were all in agreement of the decision to transfer her." She offered him a reassuring smile. "Sounds like Mr. Braun is up next to be bumped to the floor if we run out of beds."

"Yeah, okay. Thanks, Andrea." Gina hurried off as the double doors opened revealing a nurse and a tech pushing Ms. Landcaster's bed into the unit.

Her head still hurt, but she pushed the pain aside and headed over to assist Gina with getting Ms. Landcaster settled in. The resident accompanying the patient looked annoyed.

"You guys shouldn't have bumped her out."

"She was stable." Andrea kept her voice even with an effort. "We only have one open bed now, so you can understand our dilemma. Any patient who crashes up on the surgical units will end up taking our last bed."

"Yeah, well, you need to find someone else to transfer out." The resident scowled at her. "Ms. Landcaster needs to stay put."

Andrea bit back a snarky response. Everyone was tired,

tense, and crabby having to work Christmas Eve, even without the added impact of the snow emergency. Ignoring him, she connected Ms. Landcaster to the heart monitor, taking note of her tachy rhythm. The elderly woman's breathing was a tad fast, but not too alarming.

Noah hovered in the doorway, watching. He gave her a nod, then turned to head back down the hall. Likely returning to Decker's room.

Leaving Ms. Landcaster to Gina, Andrea washed her hands and walked back to the break room to get more coffee. She rubbed her sore temple. As the charge nurse for the unit, she and Noah had made the decision to transfer Ms. Landcaster together. Nurses didn't discharge patients, doctors did.

There was no point in taking the resident's annoyance personally. They were all doing the best they could under the circumstances.

Andrea glanced at the relentless snow that hadn't slowed down one iota. It was now 11:20 at night.

Eight more hours to go. Maybe longer if the stupid snowstorm didn't stop soon.

NOAH KEPT a close eye on Mr. Decker's condition. The kid's condition seemed to have stabilized. The extra fluids and additional antibiotic were doing the trick. The nurse Sam Davis was doing a good job keeping up on the patient's needs.

The bad news was that the higher doses of antibiotics were starting to impact the patient's kidneys. It was only a matter of time before he'd have to start continuous venous-venous hemodialysis, also known as CVVH.

That would mean making Decker a one-to-one patient. One nurse to handle the hourly monitoring of the CVVH machine and the patient himself. Sam had a second patient, as two patients per nurse was the typical staffing ratio. Noah turned and headed back to the breakroom to give Andrea the bad news.

He found her sitting at the breakroom table, resting her head on her arms. When he helped himself to some fresh coffee, she lifted her head and blinked at him. "Oh, hey. Ms. Landcaster is doing fine. Her condition bears watching, but it's not quite as bad as the resident made it sound."

"Figures." He grimaced. This was an ongoing battle between the general floor and the critical care units. "That only leaves one empty bed."

"I know. Mr. Braun is still doing okay, though." She yawned and sipped more coffee. "How's Mr. Decker?"

"I need to start him on CVVH." At her wince, he sighed. "I know that puts a wrench in the nursing assignments, but I don't have a choice. His kidneys aren't working as well as I'd like them to."

"I understand." She managed a smile. "I can help. Thankfully, Mr. Braun's condition is stable. His biggest complaint is that he has to stay flat on his back for another couple of hours yet."

"Sounds good." He took another long sip of his coffee. The caffeine wasn't boosting his energy as much as he'd hoped. He hadn't pulled an all-nighter in a while and had forgotten how rough they could be. He set his cup aside, eyeing the bruise darkening Andrea's skin with concern. "Let's get you another cold pack."

"No need." She waved that off and stood. "I'm fine. You'll have to place a dialysis catheter first before starting CVVH.

I'll bring the line cart down to his room and assist with the procedure."

He nodded. The sooner he got this catheter placed, the sooner they could support Mr. Decker's kidneys. And hopefully keep the kid from suffering a full-blown cardiac arrest. "Thanks."

After setting up a sterile field, Noah gowned up as Andrea did the same. She'd instructed Sam to get his second patient's cares caught up so she could take over for what was left of the night.

He eyed the monitor, then turned his attention back to the patient. The kid already had one large catheter in his subclavian vein, but he needed to place another on the other side of his chest. They needed access for both the CVVH and for the vasopressor medications, fluids, and antibiotics. After doing a brief time-out, he used his landmarks to place a new large-bore dialysis catheter without difficulty. The biggest concern during this procedure was the possible complication of a pneumothorax, accidentally puncturing a lung. Once he had the catheter in place, he watched the patient's chest rise and fall. Then he took note of Mr. Decker's oxygen saturation levels at 92 percent. He sighed in relief. No complications this time.

Andrea quickly set up the CVVH machine. Sam joined her a few minutes later. "I'm going to need help with my other patient."

"I know. I'll watch over him." Andrea didn't hesitate, even though Noah knew her patient, Mr. Braun, was on the other side of the unit. She was the kind of nurse who would always step up to support her colleague in a crisis.

He would have offered to help her out, but that was impossible. As the critical care fellow, every patient in the

ICU was his responsibility. Stripping off his gown, mask, and gloves, he tossed them into the garbage.

"Do you have the CVVH orders entered?" Andrea asked.

"Getting to that now." He gave her the parameters, then tugged Bessie over to enter the series of orders.

When he was finished, he glanced at the clock, realizing the hour was five minutes past midnight. *Merry Christmas,* he thought wearily.

An emergency three-beep alarm punctuated his thought.

Here we go again. Noah pulled Bessie out of the way as Andrea ran into the hallway. The source of the alarm was their new trauma patient, Cole Slatter. Noah was right behind Andrea as they entered the room in time to see the large man lean forward to pull his breathing tube out.

"He's a Houdini," Gretta said as she struggled to get push Cole back down on the mattress. "One minute he's out cold, the next he's sitting up and pulling out tubes!"

"You have plenty of sedation orders, don't you?" He tried not to show his frustration. "I need another intubation tray."

"I'll get it," Andrea said, ducking from the room.

"I'm sorry." Gretta looked chagrined. "He was so quiet I didn't think he'd need another dose so quickly."

He helped fit a face mask over Cole Slatter's mouth and nose. "From here on, you'll need to stay on top of those meds."

"I will." Her face flushed. "I'll get another dose of Versed now."

"Wait until I'm set up to place the tube before you give it." Noah was having a hard time keeping the face mask on as Cole thrashed his head from side to side. "I don't want him to crash before I'm ready."

Gretta nodded and headed for the medication dispensing machine. Andrea brought in the intubation cart and quickly pulled out the necessary items he'd need. He let go of the face mask, sighing when Cole shook his head again, sending the face mask flying through the air and down to the floor.

"Maybe he doesn't need the tube?" Andrea eyed Cole dubiously.

He'd considered leaving it out. Yet it didn't take long for Cole's breathing to go shallow, which corresponded with a drop in his oxygen saturation levels.

"Never mind." Andrea glanced at Gretta, who stood with a syringe in her hand. After seeing how wild Cole had been, she said, "Make sure the IV is still good."

Gretta nodded and set the syringe aside to assess the IV. "Good blood return," she announced.

Noah lowered the head of Cole's bed, pulled it from the wall so he could stand beside it, and reached for the endotracheal tube and laryngoscope. "We're placing a size eight point five endotracheal tube in patient Cole Slatter. Gretta, go ahead and give the Versed."

Gretta did so. Two minutes later, Cole finally relaxed and stopped struggling.

Noah opened the patient's airway and peered inside the mouth, looking for the vocal cords. Cole's throat was red and slightly swollen from his yanking the tube out, but he was still able to visualize the cords.

Yet he also knew that if this kid pulled out another tube, they could be in big trouble. He didn't necessarily blame Gretta for what happened, but he needed to make sure she stayed on top of his sedation moving forward.

"Okay, the tube is in," he announced. "Color change indicates correct placement." Drake, the respiratory therapist, handed him the fallen ambu bag. Noah gave the patient two slow, deep breaths as Andrea listened to the patient's lung sounds.

"Good breath sounds bilaterally," she said, pulling the stethoscope from her ears.

After securing the tube in place and getting it connected to the ventilator, he pulled off his protective gear. "Gretta, keep him sedated, okay? If he pulls out another tube, we'll be forced to do an emergency tracheotomy."

"I understand." The nurse avoided his gaze. "I said I was sorry."

"I know he's a handful." Noah slipped around the bed and headed to the computer to write his intubation note. "I'm just letting you know that his throat is red and swollen. If he extubates himself, we'll have to trach him."

"I'll grab a trach tray to have on hand if needed," Andrea said.

He nodded and finished his documentation. Maybe it wasn't fair, but he was convinced that if Andrea had been Cole Slatter's nurse, this wouldn't have happened.

Turning away, he headed back down the hall to Decker's room. The vital signs on the monitor were reassuring. Sam examined the CVVH machine with an intense expression. Noah hoped the newer ICU nurse wasn't in over his head.

Noah stopped by to check on his second sickest patient on his way back to find Andrea. He trusted her judgment when it came to her peers. As the charge nurse, she was the person to work on the patient assignments, matching them with nurses' skill levels.

She was in with Mr. Braun, who he was glad to see looked good. "Your flat bed-rest stint is over." She smiled as she lifted the head of his bed to thirty degrees. "I'll get you some more ice chips, okay?"

"Thanks. How about a cheeseburger?" The older man's eyes twinkled. "I'm hungry."

Andrea glanced at Noah, then spooned some ice chips into Mr. Braun's mouth. "Cheeseburgers aren't good for your heart," she said lightly. "But I'll talk Dr. Weston into allowing you to start with some clear liquids, like Jell-O and broth. Low-salt broth," she added when Mr. Braun's eyes lit up with anticipation.

"Yuck. Who likes low-salt broth?"

Noah stepped into the room. "Mr. Braun, I'll write the order for clear liquids, but understand this, you'll need to make some diet changes moving forward. Three of the main arteries in your heart were almost one hundred percent blocked. That's not good. You're fortunate the cardiologist was able to open them up, but that also means doing better moving forward, okay?"

"Yeah, doc. I hear you." Mr. Braun's expression turned contrite. "My wife yells at me for eating too much fast food."

"You should listen to your wife." Andrea rested her hand on Mr. Braun's arm. "Staying healthy is important. Fast food is the worst. I'll have the dietitian meet with you after the holiday, okay?"

"Okay. I want to stick around for a little while yet. I got grandkids to spoil." Mr. Braun sighed. "Bring on the Jell-O and low-salt broth."

"Coming right up." Andrea left the room, returning a few minutes later with the items. Noah followed Andrea back into the break room, intending to discuss Sam's ability to care for Mr. Decker, when she stopped abruptly, then turned to grasp his arm.

"What's wrong?" he asked in alarm.

"Look!" Her grip tightened as she gestured to the window. "It's stopped snowing!"

"Praise God," he said in a low voice. "Does that mean the snow emergency will end soon?"

"I hope so." Andrea's blue eyes were bright with anticipation. "I would love nothing more than to be home in time for the kids to open their presents and to read the story of Jesus's birth."

"You will be." He turned away, doing his best to hide the fact that while he was thrilled for Andrea, his holiday would consist of going home to an empty condo.

No holiday celebrations were in his future. Yet as he stood there, Noah realized how badly he wanted that to change. It was well past time for him to jump back into the dating pool.

He just needed to find a way to convince Andrea to give him a chance.

ndrea's excitement over the snow stopping came to a screeching halt when they learned they were getting another patient from the emergency department. Mandy Cobb, who was barely sixteen, had been found down outside in the snow. She was severely hypothermic, and while that type of patient typically went to the medical ICU, they didn't have an empty room. Which meant the patient was coming to the surgical ICU instead.

"How much time do I have?" Andrea asked the ED charge nurse Tim Stokes. "I need to transfer another patient to the floor."

"I can give you twenty minutes, but the docs down here are anxious to send her up," Tim said. "If you could call down when you're finished with your transfer, that would be great."

"Okay. Thanks." Andrea disconnected from the call and made another call to get Mr. Braun a floor bed. At times like this, it felt like they were playing musical beds. The moment one bed was taken, they needed to open another one.

Pasting a bright smile on her face, she told Mr. Braun

he'd be heading to the floor. "You're doing so well, you don't need to be here listening to all the beeping alarms. You'll get more rest in a private room on the general unit."

"That sounds good to me." Mr. Braun shifted in the bed, yawning widely. He idly rubbed his chest, as if still sore from the shocks they'd used to restore his heart rhythm. Andrea tried not to feel guilty over the decision to move him out of the ICU. It wasn't that long ago that Mr. Braun had almost died. Yet there was no denying he looked 100 percent better now that his coronary arteries had been repaired.

He'll be fine, she silently told herself. His earlier problems with his breathing were likely related to his poorly functioning heart in the first place, and that was better now.

Andrea stepped out of his room to call up to the floor nurse who would be taking over Mr. Braun's care. Five minutes later, she and a transport staff member rolled Mr. Braun out of the ICU. She'd asked for a stat clean on his empty room for their new patient, Mandy Cobb.

When Andrea returned to the unit, the housekeeping staff assigned to their floor was already at work cleaning. She took a moment to check on her other patient, the one she'd agreed to watch for Sam.

Ms. Jones was two days post liver resection and was still on a ventilator to support her breathing. They were keeping her sedated, but it would soon be time to hold the medication to see if she was strong enough to come off the vent. Andrea took a set of vital signs, repositioned her patient in the bed, then ducked out to call Tim.

"We're ready for Mandy Cobb." She winced when she saw the time was exactly twenty minutes. "Sorry I couldn't get her earlier."

"We're on our way up," Tim said. "See you soon."

She ended the call and hurried back down to the empty

room to replenish the supplies. She was still stocking items in the cart when Tim and another ED staff member wheeled Mandy into the unit.

Noah must have seen them coming down the hallway, as he was right behind them. Andrea abandoned her restocking and quickly turned her attention to the young girl on the cart. Mandy looked much younger than sixteen. Her pale, waxy features did not bode well for a good outcome.

"Do we know what happened?" Andrea glanced at Tim as she connected Mandy to the monitor. "Why was she outside? And for how long?"

"We don't know how long she was outside; the police are still investigating. Upon arrival, she was wearing a coat, hat, and gloves, so she was prepared for the weather." Tim shook his head as he adjusted the heating blanket that covered her. "The police found her car stuck in a snowbank a half mile from where she was found. They think she was walking home but got lost in the blizzard and then succumbed to hypothermia."

Andrea's heart squeezed in her chest. The scenario was too vivid in her mind. The better option would have been to stay in her car. Not that she still couldn't have ended up with hypothermia then too. "What's her core temp now?"

"Barely ninety-four degrees." Tim sighed. "She was at ninety-two-point-two when she arrived."

Ninety-two was critically low, but Andrea had seen worse cases. Patients with a core temp of lower than that rarely survived. Mandy had a chance, if they could get her temp back up to normal.

"We need a fluid warmer," Noah said. "I'm encouraged that her temp has come up a bit since arriving at the hospital, but she's not out of the woods yet."

"Will do." Andrea hurried to the storeroom to fetch the warmer. If she'd had more time to prepare, she'd have already had the machine set up and ready to go. Swallowing a sigh of regret, she quickly set the machine up at Mandy's bedside.

"She looks so young," Noah murmured as she quickly flushed the machine and began to connect the fluids to Mandy's IV. "It's crazy to think that her parents allowed her to drive in a blizzard."

"I know." Andrea couldn't imagine doing that herself, much less allowing her sixteen-year-old to drive through the storm. "The only good news is that her youth may help her recover from this."

"Most studies on patients surviving severe hypothermia are on young kids below the age of eight. Not on teenagers." Noah used his stethoscope to listen to Mandy's heart and lungs. Then he straightened. "We need to be prepared to resuscitate her."

Andrea nodded in understanding. She was surprised CPR hadn't been in progress during the transfer. Most patients with severe hypothermia suffered a cardiac arrest. Granted, in this situation, Mandy's young age worked in her favor.

The next thirty minutes passed by quickly. Andrea was grateful to see Mandy's core temp rise a half degree with the IV fluid warmer combined with the Bair Hugger external warming blanket. In severe cases, she'd seen ECMO, extracorporeal membrane oxygenation, used to treat hypothermia. She personally had only cared for one patient who had undergone that procedure. It was a mode of treatment used more often now; she just hadn't been working during the years it had gained popularity.

Swallowing hard, she tried not to think about that until

she had to. Hopefully, someone else on the unit had more experience than she did.

"No word from her parents?" Noah asked when he returned from checking on Mr. Decker.

"Not yet." She glanced at him. "According to Tim, the police were headed there to notify them of her being here."

Noah's brow hiked up. "That's interesting. They didn't report her missing? Do you think she left the house without telling them?"

She grimaced and shrugged. "I have no idea. But that makes more sense than believing her parents blithely allowed their teenager to head out in the storm."

"Especially in the middle of the night." He raked a hand through his hair, his gaze seemingly fixated on Mandy's pale face. "It's always harder to take care of kids. This is why I prefer the adult population."

"My brother Adam is a pediatrician at Children's Memorial, and his wife, Krista, is a pediatric nurse." She shook her head wryly. "Honestly, I give them both a lot of credit. I couldn't do it. Especially not after having kids of my own. Two years ago, Bethany was hit by a car and needed surgery to repair her leg fracture. That was more than enough of a traumatic event for me to handle. Just imagining taking care of sick or injured kids the same age as Bethany and Ben is enough to make me shudder."

"Me too." Noah shoved his hands into the pockets of his lab coat. "Sounds like your family is invested in the medical field."

"More than you know," she said with a weak smile. "My oldest brother, Aaron, is the chief pediatric cardiothoracic surgeon at Children's Memorial; he's married to Maggie, an anesthesiologist. My sister Amber is a nurse married to a rehab physician named Nick Tanner. My brother Austin is a paramedic/firefighter also married to a nurse, Lindsey. My other brother, Alec was a medic in the army but then went into law enforcement when he got out. At least he was smart enough to marry Jillian who is a neurologist."

Noah stared at her. "You're serious? You have that many nurses and physicians in the family?"

"Yep." She kept her tone light, despite the heaviness in her heart. To think she'd purposefully avoided marrying a physician or anyone in the medical field only to learn her husband had been a cheater.

"That's impressive." Noah stared at Mandy for another long moment. "I need to make rounds. Let me know when she reaches a core temp of ninety-six."

"I will." She watched Noah turn to leave, then pulled another bag of IV fluid out of the supply cabinet, connecting it to the warmer. Her gaze lingered on Mandy's pale face framed by her blond hair. Even with the breathing tube in place to support her lungs, she was so young, so pretty.

Andrea didn't even want to consider the possibility that this young teenager might die. Especially on Christmas Day.

Despite not leaning on prayer as much as she should have over the past eighteen months, she found herself silently praying God would spare this girl's life.

Noah had to force Mandy's sweet innocent face out of his mind as he began making rounds on his patients. It bothered him to think of losing someone so young. That thought made him think about Andrea's pediatrician brother and the fact that her entire family worked in the medical field. *Except her brother the cop*, he thought with a smile. He sensed there was more to that story than she'd let on.

But this wasn't the time to think about Andrea's family. He focused on making rounds. It wasn't something he normally did this often, but fatigue was wearing him down, and he figured it was better to round on his patients than to fall asleep in the break room.

The hours between three and five in the morning were the worst. It was as if his entire body wanted to shut down to rest. Yet despite his exhaustion, he couldn't bear to drink more coffee. His stomach was rolling enough as it was.

The sandwiches the hospital administrators had brought were long gone. He was hungry, but he didn't think there was any point to heading down to the cafeteria. It normally wasn't open in the middle of the night, and probably less so in a snow emergency.

How long would the administrators keep the snow emergency in place anyway? Now that the snow had stopped, surely some of the staff would be able to make it in. He paused to stare out at the snow-covered landscape. When he saw a small plow making its way through the medical center's streets and parking lots, he nodded in satisfaction. Turning away, he headed down to Mr. Decker's room. He'd hoped to see his counterpart Jeff Ramos by now. But in his absence, he knew these critically ill patients depended on him to get them through what remained of the night.

Blizzard or not, they deserved the best medical care possible.

Thankfully, Mr. Decker's vitals were stable. Better, really, than they had been. The continuous venous filtration was working, and for that, Noah was grateful.

By the time he made it around to Cole Slatter's room, he'd thought they were in good shape.

"Oh, I'm glad you're here." Gretta looked flustered. "Cole's pupils are unequal now, and I'm worried his head injury is getting worse."

Frowning, Noah pulled a penlight from his pocket to see for himself. The left pupil was slightly larger than the right. Swallowing a wave of concern, he quickly continued assessing the young man's neurological status.

"He's not responding well on the left side either." Noah quickly grabbed Bessie and accessed Cole Slatter's medical record. The CT scan of his head from earlier that evening showed a right-sided subdural hematoma—basically a small bleed in the right side of his brain. An injury to the right side of his brain would cause weakness on the left side of Cole's body. He looked at Gretta. "We need to get another stat CT scan of his brain. And from there, we'll have to start the hypothermia protocol." As he gave the orders, his fingers flew across the keyboard to enter them.

"Okay." Gretta didn't argue and quickly used her hands-free device around her neck to call down to radiology.

It was not lost on Noah that they would use hypothermia as a treatment modality now to decrease the impact of Cole Slatter's brain injury, while Mandy Cobb required rewarming therapy as she battled for her life across the hall.

For a moment, he wondered when Gretta had done the last neuro check on Cole. Had the young man's condition changed that much in the past hour? Or had it been a few hours since she'd checked him last?

It wasn't fair to hold the earlier incident of the patient's self-extubation against her, but he couldn't help it. Some staff nurses were just not as observant and on top of things as they should be. Yet he had to admit, these were extraordinary circumstances. Every single one of them were operating on no sleep, working for more than twenty hours straight.

Reminding himself they were doing their best, he finished the orders and returned to Mandy's room. Andrea glanced over with a smile when he walked in.

"She's up to ninety-five for a core temp." Andrea gestured to the heart monitor. "I've seen a few premature ventricular beats, but nothing terrible. I think she's going to make it."

"That's good." He wouldn't be satisfied until her temp was up to ninety-six but decided it was okay to be cautiously optimistic. "Still nothing on her parents?"

"Oh, yes, I got a call from the ER. They'll be here within ten minutes or so." Her smile faded. "This is going to be really hard on them."

He nodded. "I'll talk to them when they arrive. By the way, Cole Slatter's head injury is worse. He's heading down for another CT of his brain, then we'll start the hypothermia protocol."

Andrea groaned. "That makes him a one-to-one patient too. I'm not sure who will be able to pick up Gretta's other patient."

He understood her concern. "I'm sorry. But maybe some of the staff nurses will make it in soon to help out."

"Maybe." Andrea didn't look convinced. "Thanks for letting me know." She gave Mandy Cobb one last look, then edged past him. Despite the long shift, he caught the flowery scent that seemed to cling to her hair. He'd noticed it weeks ago and had decided it was from her shampoo.

No point in thinking about that, he mentally chided

himself. He needed to stay focused on patient care. Not his sorely lacking personal life.

He hadn't quite finished his rounds when he received the call from Andrea. "Mr. and Mrs. Cobb are here."

"Coming." He took a moment to glance into the last two patient rooms, which wasn't nearly enough to know how they were doing, before heading back to Mandy Cobb's room. The couple standing at the bedside were clearly distraught, which was understandable. Swallowing the lump that had lodged in the back of his throat, he approached. "Mr. and Mrs. Cobb? I'm Dr. Weston."

Mr. Cobb turned sunken eyes toward him as his wife sobbed softly beside him. "We heard Mandy is suffering from hypothermia. Can you tell us how she's doing now? Is she going to make it through this?"

"We consider your daughter's condition to be critical but stable. We're doing everything we can to warm her body to a normal temperature. We have warm IV fluid infusing into her blood stream and a warming blanket on top of her." Noah gestured to the monitor. "You can see there her core temp is only ninety-five point two degrees. She still has a ways to go until she reaches a normal body temperature. And we need to wait for that to happen before we can assess her neurological status." He decided not to go into detail about the frostbite on her extremities. That was the least of their concerns for the moment.

"What do you mean, her neurological status?" Mrs. Cobb lifted her tearstained face to look at him. "Are you talking about her brain?"

"Yes. The good news is that cold temperatures can preserve the brain cells." Which was exactly why they were using hypothermia as a therapeutic treatment for Cole Slatter's brain injury. "Also, Mandy's heart and lungs seem to be doing well. These are all positive signs that she'll recover from this."

"But you said she's still critical," Mr. Cobb pointed out. "You're not sure our daughter will survive this?"

"She's survived this far, and that's reassuring." He hated this part of the job, where loved ones wanted reassurances he couldn't give them. "I wish I could tell you for sure that she'll pull through this, but I can't. Nobody can. We just have to wait and see."

"Oh, Rob." Mrs. Cobb began to sob again. "I can't bear the thought of losing her. I just can't."

"She will, Eloise. We'll pray she recovers," Mr. Cobb said.

Noah tried to keep an emotional distance from the pair of grieving parents, but it wasn't easy.

Sensing his gaze, Mr. Cobb looked at Noah. "Mandy left the house without telling us. She had wanted to see her boyfriend, Kyle, earlier in the evening, but we told her no, that she couldn't go anywhere in the storm, especially on Christmas. Mandy kept saying Kyle had a gift for her, and we told her that a gift exchange could wait." He shook his head slowly. "When the police came to our door, we were shocked to realize she'd left without our knowledge."

"I'm sorry you're going through this," he said in a low voice. "But try to take heart in that she's getting the best care possible here at Trinity Medical Center."

Mr. Cobb nodded, then turned to stare down at his daughter. Noah waited another moment to make sure they didn't have more questions before turning away.

Some cases were more difficult than others. As much as he cared about all his patients, Mandy's situation hit hard. Mostly because she was so young. He couldn't imagine knowing your teenager could lose her life because she'd used poor judgment in sneaking out to see her boyfriend in the middle of the night just to receive a holiday gift.

He scrubbed his hands over his face and turned to see the last two patients he hadn't rounded on. Bessie sat in the hall, waiting. Taking the computer on wheels into the room, he logged in and checked on how things were going.

Thankfully, they were both stable. Considering how much time he'd spent on the sicker patients, that was a good thing.

As he returned to the break room, he saw a nurse bundled from head to toe in winter gear walk into the unit. When she pulled off her hat, he recognized her as Janet Durango.

"You made it!" Andrea came out of the break room to stare at her colleague in surprise. "How bad is it out there?"

"Pretty bad," Janet admitted. "But since I live near a fire station, our street was one of the first ones plowed. I figured you guys might need help."

"We do, so thank you." Andrea gestured to the census board. "We only have one empty bed, and several patients have become one-to-one's during the night."

"Happy to help. Let me get changed." Janet disappeared into the staff locker room.

"How are Mandy's parents?" Andrea asked, turning to him.

"As you'd expect." He glanced at the clock. It was now four thirty in the morning. "Do you think other staff members will start arriving soon too?"

"I hope so." She reached out to squeeze his arm. "I'm sure the plows will continue to make progress in clearing the streets. In another hour or two, we should see relief."

He covered her hand with his, wishing he could pull her close. "I pray you're right."

"Me too," Andrea admitted. They stood close for a moment until Janet returned. Then Andrea pulled away, looking flustered by their connection.

He tucked his hands into the pockets of his lab coat and turned to stare at the census board. Yawning widely, he blinked the exhaustion away. The end of this interminable day was here.

But it wasn't over yet. There was still a lot of work to do.

6

———

Knowing at least one staff member had made it in to work buoyed Andrea's spirits. Maybe she would get home in time to see her kids open presents and listen to the annual Christmas story. Yet as she gave the report to Janet on Sam's second patient, fatigue weighed her down. The only times she was up all night like this was if one of her kids were sick, generally a rare occurrence.

"Any questions, you'll have to talk to Sam." Andrea managed a weary smile. "Honestly, I've neglected this patient. It's been a little crazy with booting patients out to get new admissions in."

"I understand." Janet waved a hand. "I had this lady one day last week. I'll read through her medical record to get caught up."

"Good. You know her better than I do, then." Andrea turned to walk down to the other end of the ICU to check in on her patient, Mandy Cobb. She found Noah standing at the foot of the bed, eyeing the monitor. Mandy's parents were positioned on one side of her bed, which was good because that provided Andrea access to the patient. "I just need to listen to her heart and lungs, okay?"

Mr. Cobb nodded, but Mrs. Cobb seemed oblivious to Andrea's presence.

Mandy's heart was strong; although, as earlier, she did catch a few premature ventricular contractions. She hoped they weren't indicative of damage to the teenager's heart. A few scattered beats weren't necessarily a problem, but if her heart continued to throw them out there, the possibility of her going into a life-threatening rhythm rose exponentially.

"Her temperature is getting better," Mr. Cobb said, breaking the silence. "She's up to ninety-five point six degrees."

She nodded. "Yes, that's a good sign." She readjusted the Bair Hugger blanket so that it was covering Mandy's neck.

"I've ordered another fluid bolus to run through the fluid warmer," Noah said, looking up from Bessie's screen. "Her kidneys are keeping up nicely."

"Okay. I'll be right back." Andrea left to grab a few more bags of IV fluids from the storeroom. This time, she had to edge past the grief-stricken parents to reach the equipment.

The next hour passed in a flurry of activity. Two more staff nurses came in, but not nearly enough to cover the entire unit. They'd need at least eight more nurses to show up before Andrea would feel as if she could leave without putting patients in jeopardy.

And so far, there had been no sign of Noah's replacement either.

The hospital night-shift supervisor, Ron Hobert, came around with a cart of donuts, muffins, and coffee. Not the healthiest of breakfast meals, but Andrea was so hungry she didn't care about the extra calories.

"As soon as we see more staff members coming in, we'll lift the snow emergency," Ron said. "I know you're all anxious to get out of here."

That was a gross understatement, but she simply nodded. "Thanks. We've had three nurses show up so far. I'm hoping the rest of them will be here before the start of the next shift."

Ron nodded. "The plows are out in full force now. And we have two SUVs in our security department that we can use to pick up staff members if needed."

That surprised her, but she was glad to hear it. "Great. I'll let you know if we need help."

"Okay, I still have more food to deliver." Ron paused, frowned, and asked, "What happened to your face? Looks like you have a bruise near your eye."

She lifted a hand to the sore spot where Cole's fist had connected with her temple. She'd been so busy she'd barely remembered getting hit. "Oh, um, one of our patients got a little wild. I'm fine."

Ron frowned. "Did you fill out an accident report? That's a work-related injury, you know."

"Not yet, but I will." She knew the rules. All work-related incidents needed to be reported, even though her injury was mild enough that it shouldn't matter. "Thanks for reminding me."

Ron grimaced. "The stuff we put up with." He shook his head as he pushed the cart toward the automatic double doors. "Thanks again for your help during the blizzard."

"You're welcome." It wasn't as if she had much of a choice, but it was nice to be recognized for their efforts. She wiped powdered sugar from her mouth with a napkin, then headed back out to the unit.

The hour was close enough now to the start of the next

shift that she needed to check in on their sickest patients. The oncoming staff nurses would need to know what they were dealing with, especially those patients who'd taken a turn for the worse.

Five more nurses showed up a half hour later. Still not a full cadre of staff, but she was hopeful the rest would be there soon. Technically, the day-shift nurses didn't have to report for duty until seven o'clock in the morning. It was 6:20 now. She knew that most staff tended to get there between 6:30 and 6:45.

"Hey, am I glad to see you." At the sound of Noah's voice, she turned to see Dr. Jeff Ramos walking into the unit. She was glad Noah's colleague had arrived. At least he wouldn't be stuck here for much longer.

Unlike me, she thought with a sigh.

Her fears of being forced to stay were quickly assuaged when the rest of the nursing staff showed up as scheduled. There was only one nurse who didn't make it in, and when Andrea called the night-shift supervisor, he sent the security officer on duty to go pick her up. If that nurse thought that she'd get to stay home on Christmas Day because of the storm, she was sadly mistaken.

Andrea stood in front of the census board with Erica Jenkins, the charge nurse on the day shift. "You may have to take a patient assignment until Susy gets here."

"I know." Erica shrugged. "I'm hoping that when the attending physician gets in to make rounds with Dr. Ramos, we can move some more patients out of here."

"That would help." Andrea gave Erica a quick rundown on their patients.

"I can't believe we have a medicine overflow patient." Erica frowned. "We should send her up to the medical ICU as soon as they open a bed."

Andrea winced. "That will not look good to her parents. Besides, I suspect she's going to lose some fingers and toes due to frostbite. I've wrapped them for now, but we need a plastic surgeon to look at her."

Erica sighed. "Okay, we'll keep her for now. But if more trauma patients start rolling in, we'll need to reassess."

Andrea decided not to argue. She wasn't going to be there for the next few days, so Erica could do whatever she thought was best. "Any other questions for me?"

"No." Erica arched a brow. "I heard you're all getting paid double time for the duration of the snow emergency because it was over a holiday."

Andrea thought of the new roof fund she was slowly building in her savings account. Being a single mother now meant she needed to be careful with budgeting. Especially since Stuart hadn't had life insurance. She'd received some money from the trucking company because of the crash being the truck driver's fault, but it wasn't nearly enough to carry her family for long.

Now she was relieved to know that getting twelve hours of double-time pay would help her reach that goal. "That's great news."

"Yeah." Erica patted her back. "You look beat. Go home and get some sleep."

"With two kids opening presents on Christmas morning?" Andrea laughed. "Not likely. But thanks."

She headed to the locker room, scanning the unit for Noah. There was no sign of him, so she knew he'd probably headed home. She pulled on her winter coat, hat, boots, and gloves, before heading out to the staff parking structure. The snow had stopped, but the icy wind stole her breath.

Hunching her shoulders against the cold, she hurried along the slippery path to the structure. She'd parked on the ground level, being Christmas Eve meant there had been plenty of open spaces. Hospital policy was to leave the closest parking spots for patients and families, so she wound her way through the cars to the far corner.

Then she stopped abruptly when she saw her car was covered in snow. Between the wind blowing snow at her vehicle and the snowplow that had come through, her car was halfway buried. Mostly the front end, not the back. Still, it would take her a while to dig out. She groaned and clicked her key fob to unlock the car.

Nothing happened.

No, no, no! She wanted to scream in frustration. Andrea tried again, but there was no flash from the taillights. No chirping sound of the car unlocking.

A wave of despair had her dropping her chin to her chest. It wasn't the end of the world, one of her siblings would head out to pick her up, but after the long twenty-four-hour shift, she so wasn't in the mood for this.

No doubt this was one of the worst holidays on record.

NOAH HAD BEEN SURPRISED to learn Andrea had left before he had. He'd strode out to the staff parking lot and climbed into his Jeep. When he backed out of his parking space, he saw Andrea standing near a car that was half buried in snow. He slowed to a stop and lowered his window. "Andrea? Is that your car?"

She jerked her head up. A wry expression crossed her features. "Yeah. I thought you were already gone."

Knowing she'd looked for him made him smile. "You beat me out of there. Do you need help getting the car unburied?"

"No, the battery is dead." She frowned. "You parked here? I thought all the physicians parked in the lower level?"

"Only the attending physicians get that privilege. I'm just a lowly critical care fellow." He unlocked the doors. "Climb in. I'll drive you home."

She looked surprised by his offer. "Are you sure? I was going to call one of my siblings to pick me up." The corner of her mouth tipped up in a smile. "One of the advantages of coming from a large family."

"I'm happy to help." He couldn't deny being thrilled to have some time alone with her. "Jump in, it's cold."

After a moment's hesitation, she nodded and hurried around to get into the passenger seat. Closing the door, she settled back in the warm car. "Thanks, Noah. I really appreciate this."

"It's not a problem." He glanced at her half-buried car. "That's crazy. You'd think the snowplow service would avoid covering staff vehicles."

"Right?" She clicked her seat belt into place. When she shivered, he reached over to touch a button on the dash.

"Seat warmer," he explained. "The best invention ever."

She laughed. "My car isn't that fancy."

He glanced at her but didn't pursue the subject. As he made his way out of the parking structure, he asked, "What's your address?"

"I'm heading to my parents who live in Brookland. They moved about a year ago." She rattled off the street address. When he arched a brow, she added, "I'll give you directions. Turn left here, then head north."

Driving carefully through the recently plowed streets, he was surprised to see that many of the side roads still weren't cleared. "Looks like we got about twelve inches of snow."

"Fourteen, at least according to the weather station."

Andrea sighed and gestured to the massive snow piles left behind by the plows. "That's a lot of snow in a short amount of time."

"Yeah. I grew up in southern Missouri. We didn't have blizzards like this very often."

She tipped her head to the side. "I bet you're wishing you were back home now, huh?"

"Not really. I like the area. It's a big city, yet feels like a small town." He grinned. "And the experience of working with top-notch nurses makes it even better."

"Flattery will get you nowhere," she teased. "I'm sure the nurses in Missouri are just as talented."

He liked seeing the lighter side of Andrea Monroe. As they passed a large condo complex to the right, he gestured to it. "I live over there. It's not bad. In the summer, I bike to work."

"Nice. I have a small house about a mile from the medical center. I don't bike to work, though. It's all I can do to get out of the house on time while making sure the kids are ready to go."

He could imagine how hectic her mornings must be. There was also a part of him that envied her. She had a family, one she clearly loved and cared about.

Noah had been alone far too long.

Andrea yawned widely, then quickly covered her mouth with her hand. "Sorry about that."

"No need to apologize. I'm beat too." He glanced at her. "You won't be sleeping when you get home, huh?"

"Nope. Not with two kids who are probably already finished opening their presents." Her smile turned sad. "I'm sure they didn't miss me as much as I missed being there for them."

"Hey, they love you." He reached over to take her hand. They both wore gloves, but he didn't care. "I have no doubt they'll be thrilled to see you."

"I know you're right." She continued holding his hand. "I need to stop feeling sorry for myself. The kids are loved by my parents, their aunts and uncles, and their cousins." She bit her lower lip. "It's only one day. We'll have plenty of other holidays to spend together."

"You have a right to be sad over missing family time. Although selfishly, I'm glad you were there during the snow emergency. You made my job easy." When she looked at him in surprise, he shrugged. "I'm being honest. Some of the charge nurses aren't nearly as helpful as you are."

"Oh, well, that is the job." She looked adorably flustered. "If someone isn't pulling their weight, you should let our manager know."

"Nah, I'd rather not make trouble for anyone." Physicians relied on the nurses to be their eyes and ears. The charge nurse role required nurses to manage the patient flow within the unit. That wasn't necessarily everyone's skill set. "I just wanted you to know how much I enjoy working with you."

"Thanks. Same." She subtly tugged free of his grip and turned to look out the window.

He realized he'd come on too strong and quickly changed the subject. "So now that you have the rest of the holiday off, when do you work next?"

"Not until Monday." She smiled. "I'm glad to have the weekend off."

He did, too, but he decided not to mention it.

Andrea continued to give him directions until he pulled up in front of a two-story house with a wide porch out front.

The home was fully decorated for the holiday: icicle lights hanging from the gutters on both floors, two pine trees lit up with multicolored lights, a nativity scene was set up in the front yard, and there was even a large wreath with a big red bow hanging on the front door.

He wondered how long it had taken Andrea's parents to decorate the place. Hours at the very least. "Wow." He pulled into the snow-cleared driveway. "Looks amazing."

"Yeah, my parents tend to go overboard for the holidays." Andrea grinned. "Granted, Adam and Alec had to do most of the work. My father suffered a heart attack a few years ago, so he's been banned from climbing ladders or doing heavy lifting. He grouses about it, but I know he's secretly glad the guys are around to lend a hand. My brother Aaron would have helped, too, but he was called in for a pediatric cardiac emergency the day they were putting everything up."

"Don't you have another brother?" He tried to remember the names she'd rattled off. "A firefighter/paramedic?"

"Yes, Austin still lives in California. He and Lindsey are here for Christmas, but they weren't here when the decorating party took place." She unlatched her seatbelt. "Thanks for the ride, Noah. I really appreciate it."

"I told you, it's no problem." He didn't add that there was nothing waiting for him at the condo. Not even a cat.

Maybe he should consider getting one.

The front door opened, and two kids, an older girl and a younger boy, came barreling out of the house. "Mommy! Mommy! Santa came!"

Andrea pushed her door open and slid out to greet them. Just seeing her face light up when Bethany and Ben threw themselves into her arms choked him up. What was wrong with him anyway? He needed to get out of there and back to reality.

His reality, which didn't include Andrea or her family.

"Who's car?" A tall man with dark hair had joined the kids, along with another young girl who appeared to be a similar age to Bethany.

"Oh, this is Dr. Noah Weston. He's one of our critical care fellows." Since Andrea's door was still open, she bent down to look at him. "Noah, this is my brother Alec and his daughter, Shannon. He's a cop."

"That's Sergeant Monroe to you, sis." Alec grinned and jabbed her with his elbow. "Nice to meet you, Noah. Do you want to come in and join us for Christmas brunch? We have enough food to feed an army. And I should know since I did a six-year stint myself."

It took a second for Andrea to nod in agreement. "Actually, that's a great idea. I should have thought of that earlier. Noah doesn't have family in the area." She met his gaze. "Please join us. Just prepare yourself for a bit of chaos. My family can be, well, loud."

Noah knew that he should excuse himself to go home, but he couldn't do it. The thought of being inside his empty condo, one he hadn't even bothered to decorate for the holiday, was too depressing. He held Andrea's gaze. "Are you sure you don't mind?"

"Of course I don't mind! The more the merrier." She gestured to the house. "Come on, we need to get the kids back inside."

"Okay, thanks." Noah killed the engine and pushed out of the driver's seat. Andrea slammed the passenger door shut, then waited for him to join them.

"Mommy, we still have one present to open," Bethany

said as they headed inside. "Grandma and Grandpa made us wait for you to get home."

"Really?" Andrea stopped just inside the hallway to peel off her winter gear. Noah did the same, watching with amusement as the three kids dropped their coats on the floor.

"Hold on, put your coats away." Alec's firm voice had the three kids stopping in their tracks. With a resigned look, they bent to pick up their things. "You know where they go."

"Race you," Ben said, running down the hall to what Noah assumed was a mudroom.

The two girls rolled their eyes and walked.

"Well, who's this?" an older man with a booming voice called from the living room. "Come in, come in. Have a seat."

"Dad, Mom, this is Dr. Noah Weston. He's one of the critical care fellows from work." Andrea made the introductions. "Noah, my parents, Abe and Alice Monroe."

"So that's why all the kids have names starting with the letter A," Noah said with a smile. "Didn't that get confusing?"

"Very confusing, but it seemed like a good idea at the time. Welcome, Noah." Alice beamed. "Please have a seat. Can I get you something to drink?"

"Coffee," he and Andrea answered at the same time.

Everyone laughed, and Noah belatedly realized there were a dozen people in the room. More if you counted the kids. He hoped he could keep them all straight. Especially with all those A names.

"Noah, this is my family." She gestured as she spoke. "My brother Aaron and his wife, Maggie, and their kids Joey and Max; Adam and his wife, Krista, and their new baby, Darla; Alec and his wife, Jillian, they have Shannon; Austin and his wife, Lindsey, their son Josh and new daughter Emma; my sister Amber and her husband, Nick, and their baby, Carter. And of course, my parents." As Andrea rattled off names that he tried to put with a face, he couldn't help but think about how wonderful it was to come home to a family like this.

Which made him realize once again how lonely his life was in comparison.

7

———

As the kids who were old enough to read took turns reading the children's version of the birth of Jesus from a large hardback children's book, Andrea's eyes welled with tears. Happy tears, as she cherished this time with her family. Watching Bethany, Ben, Shannon, Joey, and Josh open their last gift was sweet. But reading the Christmas story was the best part of their Monroe family tradition. Every year she got misty eyed during the reading.

When they reached the end of the book, Ben jumped to his feet, lifting his fist over his head. "I have baby Jesus!"

She smiled at her son. "You know what to do, right?"

Ben nodded vigorously and ran over to the nativity scene. "I put baby Jesus in the manger!"

"That's right. Good job, Ben," her mother praised him.

Lindsey held her baby daughter close with Austin hovering nearby. Andrea glanced at Alec's wife, Jillian, who was six months pregnant. Her sister Amber was also pregnant, which meant there would soon be additional Monroe grandkids to help read the story of Jesus's birth.

Despite being physically exhausted from their

twenty-four-hour shift, Andrea was keenly aware of Noah sitting beside her. Oddly, he seemed at home among the family chaos. Of course, it didn't help when Alec waggled his eyebrows at her behind Noah's back, acting as if she and Noah were more than friendly colleagues.

They weren't. At least, she didn't think so. Yet having him celebrate Christmas morning with the family did make it seem as if they were closer than just friends.

Yet that didn't prevent her from scowling at Alec, shaking her head, basically telling him to knock it off.

"I can't remember the last time Children's Memorial called a snow emergency," Adam said, interrupting their exchange. "Maybe back when I was a first-year resident? We had that one big blizzard then too."

"This was my first time being mandated to stay at the hospital overnight," Noah said. "I have to say, the situation could have been worse. Everyone really pulled together to make sure patient care didn't suffer."

"We did," Andrea agreed. Then she smiled wryly. "Not that we had much of a choice. Thankfully, we were busy enough that we didn't have too much time to fall asleep."

"I'm glad you didn't try to drive home in that storm," her father said with a frown. "Too dangerous, even though we're not that far away from the hospital."

"I know, Dad." Mandy Cobb's sweet, pale face flashed in her mind. When Noah glanced at her, she knew he was thinking about their young patient too.

"By the way, Andrea, what's with the bruise on your temple?" Nick asked.

"Oh, that." She put a hand up to cover the dark discoloration of her skin. "I got too close to a rambunctious patient."

"Are you hurt, Mommy?" Ben crawled into her lap. "Should I kiss it all better?"

"I'd love that." She cuddled Ben close as he pressed a kiss to the side of his head. Her son was five going on six, and she knew he wouldn't cuddle with her like this forever. She intended to enjoy this age while she could. "Thank you, I'm all better now."

Noah's gaze seemed to cling to her as Ben settled against her. She was struck by the hint of longing reflected in his dark eyes. She wondered if he and his wife had planned on having a family before she passed away. Flustered, she looked away, feeling her cheeks grow warm. She was exhausted and likely imagining things.

"Anyone hungry for brunch?" her father asked in his loud, booming voice. "I know I am."

"Sounds wonderful," Noah said graciously. "I really appreciate you inviting me to stay."

Amber and Nick stood to head into the kitchen with Alice. "Need help?" Andrea asked. She didn't necessarily want to move, but usually everyone pitched in at these family gatherings.

"You stay put," Adam said. He and Alec rose too. "We've got this."

"Thanks." She glanced at Noah. "Maybe I should be forced to work snow emergencies more often, huh?"

Noah chuckled. "I don't know that it's worth it."

As if on cue, they both yawned widely. "Okay, maybe you're right. I feel like I've been run over by a car and kicked in the head for good measure."

He frowned and edged closer. "Is your headache getting worse?"

"It's a dull throb, and I can't really figure out if it's from being struck or because of lack of sleep and too much caffeine." She sighed and pressed a kiss to Ben's hair. "Probably all of the above."

"I wanna play." Ben wiggled out of her arms to follow his cousins and his sister into the playroom with their new Christmas presents. She knew the older kids, Josh and Joey, in particular would keep an eye on Ben. Her son adored his cousins, and she often wished Austin and Lindsey would consider moving closer to home.

But that wasn't her decision, so she let it go. They were here now, which was all that mattered.

"Your kids are cute," Noah said after a moment. It suddenly occurred to her that they were alone in the living room. Everyone else had drifted toward the kitchen to help get the food ready with the exception of the two new mothers who were off likely feeding their babies.

"Thanks. Despite everything that happened, I know I'm blessed to have them." She was embarrassed that she'd confided in Noah about Stuart's infidelity. "I wanted to hate Stuart for what he did, but he also gave me Bethany and Ben, so I can't seem to hold on to my anger for long."

"He was an idiot for cheating on you." Noah's dark eyes hardened for a moment, then he abruptly stood. "Can you point me to the bathroom?"

"Down the hall on your right." She pushed herself up too. Sitting for too long made her want to close her eyes, lean back, and drift off. It was probably better for her to stay awake as long as possible so she could get back on a regular sleep pattern. "More coffee?"

"I shouldn't." He grimaced. "I'm jittery enough. Good thing I don't have to perform any medical procedures."

"I hear you." She stretched, watching him as he disappeared down the hall. As she turned toward the kitchen, her sister Amber came out.

"I like him," Amber said in a low voice. "And I'm glad you're finally moving on from Stuart's passing."

"We're friends, that's all." Andrea tried not to think about their near kiss in the break room. "He's a nice guy, but you know I don't date doctors."

"That's the stupidest rule I've ever heard. I'm married to a doctor and so is Alec and Aaron for that matter." Amber flashed an exasperated look. "It's the person inside that counts, not their career choice."

Her sister had a point, but Andrea wasn't in the mood to hear it. "We're friends," she repeated firmly. "I don't even know if he plans on sticking around after his fellowship is finished. He only has six months to go before he's an attending physician. He can get a job anywhere in the country."

"He could get a position here at Trinity Medical Center too." Amber held her gaze. "Especially if you give him a reason to stay."

Suppressing a sigh, she turned away. Her siblings knew about Stuart's affair, but they didn't know he'd planned to divorce her. They'd kept the truth from their parents, though, not wanting to add to their stress.

Besides, Stuart's betrayal didn't much matter now. He was gone. And she wasn't going to tell her children about what their father had done either.

But as Noah joined them at the large dining room table that was jam-packed with food, she couldn't help but think that Amber was right about one thing: A man's character mattered more than his profession.

Noah radiated strength and confidence, but he was also down to earth and not overly impressed with himself. And maybe, just maybe, it was time for her to realize Noah was different from the other doctors who'd flirted with her.

That maybe their friendship could turn into something more.

NOAH HID another yawn behind his hand, then bowed his head as Abe Monroe said grace.

"Heavenly Father, we thank You for bringing our family together on this glorious day of Your birth. We also thank You for keeping everyone safe in Your care during the storm. We are grateful for this food we are about to eat and ask that You continue to bless us and keep us safe. Amen."

"Amen," Noah and the other siblings echoed. He was impressed by how close the Monroe family was. Granted, the number of kids milling about was chaotic, just as Andrea had warned. Yet he had to admit, there was nothing better than having kids running around on Christmas Day.

The food was delicious, and Alec had been right, there was more than enough to go around. He couldn't imagine having family meals like this on a regular basis. Yet since so many of them were in the medical field, he sensed it was unique to have them all there at the same time.

Case in point, Andrea almost hadn't made it.

"So how was it working during the snow emergency?" Amber asked. Her gaze bounced from him to Andrea. "Must have been difficult."

"It was long," Andrea agreed. "I never worked a full twenty-four-hour shift like that before. And of course, we kept getting admissions, which meant we had to bump patients out of the ICU to make room."

"Yikes." Adam winced. "I can imagine that didn't go over well with the floor staff."

"It didn't," Noah said with a sigh. "And we had one

patient bounce back in a few hours later. Thankfully, she did okay, but the floor nurses were not happy with us."

"We ended up taking a medicine overflow patient too." Andrea held Noah's gaze for a long moment, then turned back to her siblings. "We had some difficult patient situations to deal with, but as Noah mentioned earlier, everyone pulled together to make the most of it."

"That's impressive," Abe said. "I give you a lot of credit, Andrea. I'm sure it wasn't easy to know you were missing family time."

"It wasn't, but I'm here now." She leaned over to glance at the kids' table set up in the adjoining room. "They didn't miss me as much as I missed them."

"That's how it is with cousins," Austin said. "Josh was so thrilled to know we'd be here for the holiday."

"I'm glad they had their cousins to distract them." Andrea's arm brushed Noah's as she reached for the platter of grilled potatoes. "These are the holidays they'll remember for the rest of their lives."

Noah didn't have much to contribute as talk turned toward family events. Obviously, the two pregnant women would be giving birth over the next few months, and there was already discussions about getting together again for Easter.

When the meal was over, he helped clear the table with the rest of them. It was downright comical how they kept bumping into each other. The elder Monroe home wasn't that large, and they didn't all fit in the kitchen at the same time.

"Let's form an assembly line," Andrea said. "We'll pass dirty plates into the kitchen for those closest to the sink to stack."

"She always was the bossy one," Alec muttered.

Andrea shot him a narrow glare. "That's because you were always the wild child, avoiding chores and basically causing trouble wherever you go."

"I can see that about you," Noah teased as he handed Alec a platter of leftovers. "You have that wild-child edge."

Alec grinned and shrugged. "That was then. I've changed since then." He gazed at his wife, Jillian, for a moment. "I've learned family is everything."

"Jillian was always too good for you," Andrea teased.

The ribbing went on during the entire clean-up process. Once the table was cleared, Amber and Nick washed and dried the dishes, shooing him and Andrea out of the way. "No offense, but you both look like a stiff wind would blow you over," Amber said.

"I feel that way," Andrea admitted. "Thanks, sis. I owe you one."

"Nah, but don't think I won't take you up on a babysitting offer once our baby is born." Amber patted her rounded stomach. "Between Carter and the new baby, I'll be busy."

"Deal. I don't mind babysitting at all." Andrea gave her sister a hug, then led the way back into the living room. Noah followed, his gaze lingering on the massive Christmas tree tucked into the corner of the room. He'd thoroughly enjoyed his time here, but now that the meal was over, he knew it was time for him to head home. He'd already stayed longer than he'd intended.

"Dad, can we go outside to play in the snow?" Josh asked Austin. "You said we could after brunch."

"Yeah, please?" Bethany added. "Josh doesn't get to play in the snow very often. We want to make a snow fort!"

Noah noticed the Monroe siblings glanced at each other for a moment before eventually nodding in agreement. "You'll need to bundle up," Andrea cautioned. "It's really cold outside. I don't want you to stay out too long, okay?"

"I'll head out with them," Alec offered.

"Me too," Austin chimed in with a grin. "I don't get to play in the snow very often anymore either."

"Okay!" The kids made a mad dash to the mudroom to pull on their winter gear. The sound of their excited voices made Noah smile. They were certainly excited to be spending time together.

Andrea glanced at him as they followed. "I know this is different, but I can't seem to get Mandy's face out of my mind," she said softly. "I don't want the kids to suffer from hypothermia either."

"I know, but they'll be okay outside for a short while." He flashed a reassuring smile. "They're not going to get lost for one thing. Besides, I know you and your siblings will keep an eye on them."

"Yep." She yawned again, then frowned when he reached for his coat. "Oh, are you leaving?"

"Yes." He shouldn't have been secretly happy to see the look of disappointment cross her features. "I don't want to intrude on your family time."

"You're not. Although I'm sure you're wishing for some peace and quiet right about now." She smiled wryly. "I told you it would be a little nutty here."

"It's been wonderful. The best Christmas I've had in years." He was being honest about that. "I loved spending time with your family, chaos and all. Thanks for inviting me."

"Of course." She blushed, then glanced over to where her parents were seated on the sofa. "My family enjoyed meeting you too."

Noah pulled on his coat, then turned to head back into

the living room. "Mr. and Mrs. Monroe, I need to head home but wanted to thank you again for brunch. Everything was delicious. I appreciate you having me."

"You're welcome." Alice beamed at him. "We're always happy to have our kids' friends join us."

Deep down, Noah wished he was more than Andrea's friend, but he didn't say anything.

Abe lumbered to his feet and held out a hand. "You're welcome anytime, Noah." His robust voice made Noah smile. "Take care of yourself out there."

"I will, sir. Thanks again." He turned away, doing his best to ignore the flash of regret at needing to leave. The welcoming atmosphere within the Monroe family was more than he'd anticipated. And if he were honest, he would have rather stayed for the rest of the day.

"You're leaving?" Alec asked. When he nodded, Andrea's brother glanced at her, then back to him. "Thanks for driving Andrea home."

"Of course. It was no problem." He managed a smile. "I appreciate being included in your celebration."

Alec eyed him for a moment, then grinned. "You fit in pretty well, Noah. I hope Andrea gives you a chance."

The comment caught him off guard. Did Alec mean what he thought he did? Was Andrea's brother encouraging him to ask his sister out for a date?

A better question was, would she agree if he did?

As he followed the horde of kids spilling out of the house and into the yard, he realized he didn't have Andrea's phone number. He reached out to snag her arm, drawing her off to the side. The kids ran into the backyard, and he was glad to note there were trees along the back of the property that helped to shelter them from the wind.

Feeling awkward, he cleared his throat. "Andrea, since

you're off this weekend, would you and the kids be interested in attending Winter Fest on Saturday? They're doing ice sculptures along with other fun activities I'm sure your kids would enjoy." As much as he would have preferred spending time with Andrea alone, he felt certain she'd respond better if this was a family activity.

"Really?" She cocked her head to the side, then slowly nodded. "You know, that sounds like fun." She surprised him by smiling with appreciation. "The kids would love to attend Winter Fest. And I would too," she quickly added. "We've never been there before."

"Great." He was a little surprised she'd never taken the kids to the festival before and wondered if that was something her husband hadn't been interested in. He despised the guy for cheating on her. No woman deserved to be treated that way.

Shoving that thought aside, he was thrilled she'd agreed to attend with him. He hesitated, then added, "You have my cell number from work, right? Why don't you call me tomorrow sometime? We'll figure out what time works best for the kids. I'm flexible."

"I do have your number," she confirmed. He knew the nurses had most of the physicians' personal phone numbers since that was the easiest way to get ahold of them. Paging worked, too, but he had made sure the SICU nurses could contact him at any time for any reason. "I'll let you know. Thanks again for the ride home, Noah."

"Anytime." He longed to pull her in for a hug but managed to find the strength to turn away. Now wasn't the time to push his luck. The fact that she'd agreed to attend Winter Fest was more than he'd hoped for. Did this count as a date?

He thought so, but it was her opinion that mattered.

Whatever. Just knowing he'd see her again soon made him grin as he rounded the corner of the house to his car. The kids were screeching loudly as snowballs began to fly. He couldn't help but glance back over his shoulder to see Josh nailing Alec squarely in the chest.

"I'm gonna get you for that," Alec teased, scooping snow into his gloved hands. "This means war!"

"No! Stop!" Josh shrieked as a snowball hit him in the back. Soon there was snow flying back and forth as the rest of the kids jumped into the fray.

Even Andrea joined in. As he watched, she gathered all the kids together, encouraging them to gang up on their uncle Alec.

"Hey, that's not fair!" Alec shouted, ducking as he was pelted by a flurry of snowballs.

Noah had to force himself to ignore his desire to join the family snowball fight. With a smile, he turned and made his way around to his car.

Thinking again that this was the best Christmas he'd had in a very long time.

8

Saturday morning, Bethany and Ben were fighting to the point Andrea seriously considered canceling their—what, date? With Noah. After getting some badly needed sleep, she'd alternated between looking forward to the outing and wondering what had gotten into her that she'd agreed to go out with Noah in the first place.

She'd told herself that it wouldn't hurt to have Noah as a friend.

"Mo—om," Bethany whined.

Her already frayed temper snapped. "Stop it right now or we're not going to Winter Fest." Her *I'm-not-kidding* mom voice had both kids turning to look at her. "I mean it."

"Ben keeps messing with my stuff," Bethany complained. "Tell him to play with his own toys."

"I do not," Ben shot back.

"Enough." Andrea narrowed her eyes. "You decide right now if you want to go to the festival or stay home."

Bethany sighed but didn't say anything more. Ben, too, remained silent. A moment later, both kids went their own ways. Ben was preoccupied with his new remote control car that he'd gotten for Christmas, while Bethany went back to her new chemistry set.

These were the times she hated being a single mother. Yet if she were honest, Stuart was gone so much he had never been much help when it came to disciplining the kids. That job had fallen to her. As well as handing the school homework, coordinating repairs on the house, and pretty much running things day to day.

Leaving Stuart plenty of time to find a younger woman on the side. The jerk.

Rubbing her aching temple, Andrea poured herself more coffee. The bruise had spread and was turning a darker shade of purple. Yesterday, she'd tried covering it with makeup, but that hadn't worked as well as she'd hoped. Since this little outing with Noah wasn't a date, she'd decided not to worry about it.

Not. A. Date.

Thankfully, the kids were well behaved over the next hour as she cleaned up the kitchen and finished the laundry, conscious of the fact that Noah would be there soon to pick them up. Her brothers Alec and Adam had gone to the hospital to dig out her car. They'd also replaced her battery, which was nice.

As the hour approached ten thirty, she quickly changed into a green cable-knit sweater, knowing the color matched her eyes. She added a little mascara, then caved in to the need to try covering the bruise. The foundation made the discoloration slightly less noticeable.

Good enough. She returned to the living room just as the front doorbell rang. Taking a deep breath to quell her fluttering nerves, she crossed over to answer it.

"Hi, Noah." She stepped back. "Please come in."

"Thanks." He glanced around her cluttered but mostly clean home. "Nice place."

"Who are you?" Ben asked, staring up at him.

"My name is Noah. We met on Christmas Day, remember?" Noah went down on one knee to be at Ben's level. "I work with your mom at the hospital."

Ben scrunched up his face. "Oh yeah. I remember."

"Hi." Bethany came over to join them.

"Nice to meet you both again," Noah said with a warm smile. "Are you ready to go to Winter Fest?"

"Yep! We were good, so Mommy said we could go." Ben turned toward her. "Right, Mom?"

"Right." She managed a wry smile. "It was touch and go for a while there."

Despite not having kids of his own, Noah seemed to understand. "You're going to listen to your mom while we're at the festival, okay?"

"Okay!" Ben jumped from one foot to the other. "Can we go now?"

"Yes, let's get you bundled up." She opened the coat closet, wishing she had a mudroom like her parents. The temperature outside wasn't as cold as Christmas, but she'd already told the kids they needed to wear their snow pants, boots, coat, hat, and mittens.

"Did you check in with your colleagues, yesterday?" Andrea asked as the kids got ready.

"Yes." He held her gaze. "Mandy Cobb is doing better. She's starting to wake up and seems to be over the hump as far as her hypothermia episode." He sobered. "Unfortunately, she'll lose many of her fingers and toes as a result of the frostbite. She still has a long road to recovery ahead of her."

She nodded. "I can imagine it won't be easy. But the good news is that prosthetics have come a long way over the years. She should be able to live a full life, despite the loss."

"I agree. Her parents are grateful. Teenagers, well." He shrugged. "It won't be easy for her."

"Better that than dead." Andrea glanced at her kids, who were still pulling on their winter gear. Hard to imagine losing a child at any age. She reached for her coat, hat, and gloves. "Thanks again for the invite."

"I'm glad you were able to come along." Noah smiled. "Did you really threaten to call it off?"

"Yes." She sighed. "You haven't seen them at their worst. Trust me, it wasn't pretty."

"You're an amazing woman, Andrea." Noah's low voice sent a shiver of awareness zipping down her spine.

"Not really." She cleared her throat and turned to the kids. "Are you ready to go?"

Ben and Bethany nodded. She tugged Ben's hat on tighter, then hustled the kids out the front door to where Noah had parked his Jeep.

"Hold on, I need Ben's booster seat." She detoured toward the garage. Noah came over to help. When she pulled the booster seat from her vehicle, Noah took it from her.

"I've got it." He carried the booster seat to his Jeep. Five minutes later, the kids were buckled in the back seat, and they were on their way.

The festival was set up along the rocky shore of Lake Michigan. The traffic was congested as they approached, and it took Noah a few minutes to find a parking spot.

"I hope you don't mind walking." He glanced at her. "I don't think we're going to get much closer."

"This is fine." She grinned. "The more tired the kids get by the time we're finished here, the better."

He chuckled and pushed out of the car. "Hold on to my hand, Ben."

To Andrea's surprise, Ben did. Ridiculous tears pricked her eyes at the thought that it should have been Ben's father here spending time together as a family. Stuart had been a good father, but she could count on one hand how many family things they'd done together.

With a determined effort, she pushed the thought away. She didn't get out that often either, so she was determined to make the most of it.

"Wow, look at those ice sculptures," Bethany said in awe. "They're huge!"

"They are," Andrea agreed.

"How do they make them?" Ben asked.

"First, they freeze a large block of ice," Noah explained patiently. "Then they use a hammer and a chisel to carve the ice into a shape. When that part is done, they melt some of the icy edges to make them smooth." Noah nodded toward a display table. "Look, there's someone showing how it's done now."

"Can we watch? Can we?" Ben was jumping up and down again. Noah didn't seem to mind.

"If your mom says we can." Noah winked at her. "What do you think? We can watch for a while, then get some hot chocolate."

"Sounds good." Bethany skipped alongside Noah and Ben as they headed over. Andrea couldn't help being impressed with Noah's ability to relate to her kids. Granted, a brief outing wasn't the same as listening to them fight over their toys for twenty minutes straight. Still, she was glad her kids were behaving themselves. And she found herself watching the demonstration with interest.

They wandered through the ice sculptures on the way to the hot chocolate stand. Andrea rummaged in her purse, but Noah waved that away. "My treat. It wouldn't have been nearly as much fun coming here alone."

She arched a brow, not buying he'd have come here alone for a hot minute, but she decided not to argue.

"Be careful, it's hot," she warned as she handed Ben a cup. The hot chocolate was topped with whipped cream, and her son didn't hesitate to lick it right off.

"Yum." He grinned with whipped cream–stained lips. "It's not hot."

Andrea rolled her eyes and guided both kids to a picnic table. The lakefront was crowded, but not so bad they couldn't find a seat. The wind coming off the lake was chilly, and by the time she sipped her own hot chocolate, the cold air had cooled it down.

"Mom, look!" Bethany tugged on her arm. "Sparklers! Like we had at Fourth of July! I've never seen anyone playing with sparklers in the winter."

"They're pretty," Andrea agreed.

"We'll go there next." Noah looked as if he were enjoying himself. "After we finish our drinks."

Ben was finished first and ran around the picnic table, his arms spread wide. "I'm an airplane, vroom."

Bethany put her foot out to trip him. But then she realized Noah was watching and quickly pulled it back.

Andrea sighed and wondered how long they'd behave.

"Ready for sparklers?" Noah asked.

"Yeah!" Ben finished another lap, then darted off to where there were other kids playing with sparklers. Bethany was hot on her brother's heels, leaving Andrea and Noah to follow more slowly.

"They're great kids," he said.

She snorted a laugh. "Yeah, on their best behavior because of you. Trust me, they have their moments."

He shrugged. "They're probably just missing their dad."

She shook her head. "Bethany does a little, but Ben hardly mentions him at all. Stuart wasn't home very often, and even when he was, we didn't do fun stuff like this. At least, not often enough," she hastily added.

"His loss," Noah said. He caught her hand, squeezing it gently.

"I know." She swallowed against the lump in her throat. As always, thinking about what her deceased husband had done made her sad. Her anger had faded into acceptance, but there were still times when it bothered her. "He threw his family away for a younger woman. And that choice killed him. He shouldn't have been on the highway at midnight, driving her home."

"He didn't deserve you," Noah said softly. "Like I said, his loss."

"Thanks." She knew he was just trying to make her feel better. They reached the sparkler display, and Noah didn't hesitate to buy an entire box. He lit one for each of her kids, then handed her one. He held one too.

As Bethany and Ben ran around, making letters in the sky with their sparklers, he put his arm around her shoulder and drew her close. "I'd like to see you again, Andrea. Maybe for dinner one night?"

She pulled back to look up at him. She was about to ask if he was sure about seeing her when he leaned down and kissed her.

For a moment, the winter festival activities around them

faded. It was just the two of them, standing near the frozen lakeshore. His kiss sparked a longing she hadn't realized she'd felt in Stuart's absence. She loved her kids but now understood that being a mother alone didn't fill the emptiness inside.

She liked Noah more than she should. And deep down, she wanted to see him again.

"Mom, look!" Ben's shout had Noah breaking off their kiss. He hoped he hadn't overstepped and tried to assess if he needed to apologize. "I can write my name in the air!"

"That looks amazing, Ben," Andrea called, her cheeks flushed pink. She didn't look at him, and she didn't respond to his invitation either. His heart sank. Maybe she wasn't as interested as he'd thought.

"Can we have another sparkler?" Bethany asked. As far as Noah could tell, neither kid had noticed their kiss. Which was probably a good thing. "I want to write my name too."

"Of course. I have more right here." Noah pulled two more sparklers from the pack and lit them for the kids. He noticed Andrea held her glowing sparkler close, gazing into the light with an intense gaze. Was she considering his dinner invitation?

Or was she trying to come up with a way to let him down gently?

"Help! Someone help!" a panicked voice interrupted his thoughts. He turned to see a woman kneeling on the ground beside an older man.

Without hesitation, Noah rushed over. He stuck his sparkler in the snow, as did Andrea, who had come with him. "What's wrong? Did he fall?"

"He complained his chest was hurting, then he collapsed." The woman appeared to be in her early sixties, the gentleman lying on the ground a few years older. "I was trying to get him back to the car when he went down."

Before Noah could tell Andrea to call 911, he noticed she had her phone up to her ear and was already speaking with the dispatcher. He turned his attention toward the older woman. "What's his name?"

"Ralph. Ralph Horner. I'm Wendy, his wife."

"Ralph, can you open your eyes for me?" Noah leaned over the prone male. Ralph groaned, his eyelids fluttering open.

"Hurts," he croaked, lifting a gloved hand to his chest.

"I know, help is on the way." Noah tugged off his gloves to feel for a pulse. It was weak and irregular. He felt certain the older man was suffering an acute myocardial infarction, but it was hard to know for sure without his stethoscope or any monitoring equipment at hand to see his underlying heart rhythm. "Wendy, do you have any baby aspirin with you?"

"No. Should I try to find some?" Wendy looked worried. He glanced at Andrea, who was still on the phone. She shook her head, indicating she didn't have any either.

"No, just stay here with your husband." Noah caught Ralph's gaze. "When did the pain start?"

Ralph groaned again. "On and off. Since—Christmas."

"He started shoveling our driveway, but then stopped." Wendy's expression was full of concern. "I told him to wait until the neighbor kid came home. We usually pay Jimmy to clear the sidewalks and driveway, but he was gone to his grandparents for Christmas."

"Ambulance is on the way," Andrea said. "ETA less than five minutes."

"Thanks, Andrea. Wendy, does your husband have a history of heart trouble?" Noah kept his gaze focused on Ralph, worried he'd go into full-blown cardiac arrest before the ambulance arrived. It wouldn't be the first time he and Andrea had performed CPR, but he was hoping the ambulance would get there with some medication to help avert the impending crisis.

"Not that I know of." Wendy's eyes filled with tears. "You think he's having a heart attack?"

"Hard to say for sure but maybe." Noah was vague on purpose, unwilling to upset them further. "Just relax. We're going to get you to the hospital very soon."

The red and white lights of the ambulance flickered in his peripheral vision. Andrea stood, waving them over. Less than a minute later, a pair of EMTs joined them with a gurney and a tool box full of supplies.

"Let's get him some nitro and a baby aspirin," he ordered. "And provide oxygen at two liters per minute."

"Hi, Noah." The female EMT's name was Jasmine, and he'd met her just two weeks ago when the ambulance had been called to his condo complex. "I'm surprised to see you here."

"Yeah, me too. Looks like your crew covers a wide area." Noah reached over to help connect Ralph to the heart monitor. "Let's see what we're dealing with."

"Frequent PVCs," Andrea said. She glanced at him, then added, "Too many."

"Do you have any amiodarone?" he asked Jasmine. "I'd like to start a bolus to keep him from going into full-blown v-tach."

"We don't carry that," the male EMT said. His name was Bart. "Only paramedic rigs do."

"What does that mean?" Wendy asked fearfully. "Is Ralph going to die?"

"He's holding his own," Noah assured Wendy. "The oxygen and medication are helping him already. These EMTs will get him to the hospital very soon where he'll get the best care possible."

"Okay, thank you." Wendy seemed to relax a bit.

He helped the EMTs lift Ralph onto the gurney, then stood back as they strapped him down. Jasmine sent him a flirty smile as they rolled Ralph away. He ignored her, thinking about the patient instead. If he'd been alone, he would have ridden along to offer his expertise. Not that there was anything more he could do without amiodarone.

Making a mental note to address adding the medication to EMT rigs, he turned toward Andrea. She was calling her kids over. They had spent the past few minutes playing with their sparklers, seemingly not noticing the commotion surrounding the medical emergency.

"If you want to go, I can call a rideshare to get home," Andrea offered.

"What? No. Ralph and Wendy are in good hands." He pulled on his gloves and cupped Andrea's elbow. "I'm hungry. It's time to grab something for lunch."

"Okay." This time, she didn't argue or reach for her purse, which was nice.

There were three food trucks parked along Lake Shore Drive catering to different types of foods from Mexican tacos to Greek gyros.

"I want chicken tenders," Ben announced.

"You're so lame," Bethany said with a sneer. "You can have chicken tenders anytime. I want a taco."

"How about a hot dog?" Andrea suggested after

checking the menu to see the food trucks did not have chicken tenders.

"Okay," Ben agreed.

They ate at another picnic table, then finished the day with cookies that looked like snowmen. By the time they took the long walk back to his car, Ben was lagging behind.

"Would you like a piggyback ride?" Noah went down on one knee. "Climb up."

Ben did so, clasping his arms tightly around Noah's neck. It was almost impossible to breathe, so he hiked the boy's weight up a bit, which helped ease the pressure.

Getting everyone bundled back into the car didn't take long. Ben was tuckered out, his eyes drifting shut as Noah drove back to Andrea's house.

"Thanks for the fun day," Bethany said when he pulled into the driveway.

Ben lifted his head and rubbed his eyes. "We're home?"

"Yes, Ben." Andrea slid out of the passenger seat to help get Ben's booster seat. "Say thank you to Dr. Noah."

"Thank you," Ben repeated. "I had lots of fun too."

"You're welcome." Noah wished he could have a few minutes alone with Andrea. He got out of the car and walked with them to the door.

"Thanks again." Andrea pushed the door open and encouraged the kids to go inside. He was a little disappointed she didn't invite him in. "I'll see you at work next week."

"I'm scheduled tomorrow, so I'm not working on Monday. But maybe Tuesday?" He tucked his hands into his pockets. "Think about dinner, okay?"

She looked away, then sighed. "I don't usually date doctors."

"I heard." He didn't back down. "But I think you should give me a chance."

"Maybe." The corner of her mouth tipped up in a smile. "I'll think about it. Take care, Noah." She stepped into the house and closed the door behind her.

He turned away, trying to be encouraged by the fact that she didn't turn him down outright.

The more time he spent with Andrea and her kids, the more he wanted to see her again.

9

———

The rest of Andrea's weekend went by quickly. Church services on Sunday morning, then a large family brunch with only half the siblings in attendance as Adam, Aaron, and Alec were all working. Her sister Amber noticed that she was preoccupied and guessed correctly that her thoughts were swirling around Noah and his dinner invitation.

"The kids mentioned having fun at Winter Fest," Amber said, her gaze teasing. "Sounds like Noah is a keeper."

"We're friends and colleagues." Andrea narrowed her gaze. "Don't make a bigger deal out of it than it is."

Amber rolled her eyes, but then her expression turned serious. "Listen, I know Stuart hurt you very badly. He was a jerk, but don't let one bad experience prevent you from moving on with your life. You deserve so much more. And so do your kids."

Her sister's comment touched her heart. "Maybe, but trusting men isn't exactly high on my list these days."

"It's understandable, once burned twice shy and all that. But honestly, Noah doesn't strike me as the untrustworthy type." Amber smiled. "We all noticed that he constantly watched you at Christmas. He's very interested."

She felt herself flush. Deep down, it was nice to think Noah was interested. "Stuart was attentive, too, while he was home. I didn't suspect a thing."

Amber hesitated, frowned, then said, "If you want the truth, he always seemed a little preoccupied to me. Like his thoughts were elsewhere, not on you and the kids."

"Really?" Amber's comment surprised her.

"Yes. Not that I suspected him of cheating, but I never really thought he was as committed to family time as he should have been. In my opinion, he never tried very hard to prioritize you and the kids." Her sister shrugged. "That's my two cents. I'm not sure if any of the guys noticed."

"I didn't notice." Andrea wondered if there were other signs of Stuart's infidelity that she'd missed.

"I feel bad for what you've gone through, but as the pastor at church said, everything happens for a reason. God has a plan for you." Amber lightly touched her arm. "Just make sure you're open to what God has in store for you, Bethany, and Ben."

She sighed. "I'll try. Noah invited me out for dinner. That means getting a babysitter for the kids."

"I'll babysit." Amber's eyes gleamed. "Anything to help you get back into the dating scene."

"See, that's just it!" Andrea threw her hands up. "I don't really want to be in the dating scene."

"It's dinner. Not a proposal." Amber patted her arm. "Say yes. Bethany likes helping with Carter, and Nick and I don't mind watching the kids. We'll have fun."

Andrea knew that much was true. Bethany didn't need dolls anymore now that she had so many babies in the family to help care for. And the kids wouldn't miss her as much as she'd miss them.

"Thanks. I'll talk to Noah." That was the most she would commit to for now. No matter what Amber said, she knew full well that having dinner with Noah was very different from a friendly get together at Winter Fest with the kids.

There would be no denying dinner was a real date. And she just wasn't sure she was ready to break her rule on dating doctors.

Okay, maybe Noah was one of the good ones. Like her brothers Adam and Aaron. Or her brother-in-law Nick. Logically, she knew any man could decide to cheat. Stuart was a prime example after all. It was just that doctors were surrounded by pretty nurses every day. Look how close she and Noah had gotten during the snow emergency? That was exactly the type of emotional connection that could lead to infidelity.

By Monday morning, Andrea's gut was tangled in knots over the decision of whether she should go on a date with Noah. Which was ridiculous, really. Most women didn't stress over this kind of thing.

Then again, she had her kids to consider. The last thing she wanted to do was start dating someone that Bethany and Ben got attached to, only for things not to work out. Then she remembered Alec had tried not to date Jillian for the same reason, to protect his daughter, Shannon.

And now they were married and expecting their second child, after Jillian had officially adopted Alec's daughter.

Whatever. She was getting way ahead of herself. It wasn't until she walked into the surgical ICU that she recalled Noah saying he wasn't working on Monday. Disappointment stabbed deep, but she ignored it as she headed into the break room to start her day.

Her phone dinged with an incoming text from Noah. *Have a good day.*

She couldn't help but smile as she pushed the phone back into her pocket and turned her attention to the census board. She was once again listed as the charge nurse, so she spent a few minutes chatting with the night-shift charge nurse about which patients were the sickest and those who were likely to be sent to the floor.

"You look happy," Sandy said as they finished going though the patient assignments.

Realizing she still wore a goofy smile on her face from Noah's text, she ducked her head. "Oh, well, I'm thinking about how I'll have extra money after the snow emergency to put toward my new roof."

"I don't envy you having to work through that," Sandy said. "I'm sure that was tough."

Not as difficult as it could have been if Noah hadn't been the critical care fellow on duty. But of course, she didn't say that. "It wasn't bad. And I did get some family time with the kids when it was over."

Before Sandy could say anything more, the rest of the nurses began to trickle in. Soon they were all busy getting report from the off-going shift and getting things done. Andrea took a few minutes to peek in on Mandy Cobb, moments before the plastic surgery team wheeled her to the operating room for another debridement procedure on her fingers and toes. From the distressed expression on the young girl's face, she was having trouble coming to grips with the seriousness of her condition.

Noah was right, Mandy had a long road to recovery ahead of her.

The twelve-hour shift went by surprisingly fast. Being busy helped. She was on her way out to her car, twenty minutes late because one of their patients had crashed at shift change, when Noah called. Flustered, she answered, "Hi, Noah."

"Hi, how was your shift?" He sounded casual, as if they talked on the phone on a regular basis.

Which technically they did, but not like this. Not after the workday was over.

"It was fine. A little nutty toward the end of the day." She pinched the phone between her ear and her shoulder as she dug her keys from her purse. "Just heading home now."

"Oh, I thought you'd be home already. Sorry about that. Do you want me to call back later?"

"Ah, that's okay." She winced, knowing she sounded like a doofus. It was just—she hadn't anticipated this. "I'm not in my car yet."

"I was wondering if you'd be interested in dinner tomorrow night after work? You have off on Wednesday, right?"

"I am off Wednesday." She slid into her car and started the engine, shivering a little as she waited for it to warm up. "That sounds fine, but I need to make sure my sister Amber can watch the kids overnight."

"I understand, and if it doesn't work tomorrow, we can try another time. I just thought since we were both working, it would be easier to go out afterward. You know, in case things get crazy like they did today."

He had a point. "I'll talk to my sister tonight and let you know, okay?" She could hardly believe she was going to do this. "Thanks for calling. I'll see you in the morning."

"Yep, sounds good. Have a good night, Andrea." Noah ended the call, but she continued to hold her phone pressed to her ear for several seconds longer before tucking the device into her purse.

She'd just agreed to her first date in over twelve years. She'd dated Stuart for two years prior to getting married. They'd just celebrated their eighth wedding anniversary when he'd died.

It was hard to think of herself as a single woman. *A single mom*, she hastily corrected. The other good thing about going to dinner after work was that she wouldn't have to let the kids know she was going out. They could just stay with Amber and Nick without being any wiser.

Obviously, she'd have to ask Amber about keeping the kids, but she knew her sister would be jumping for joy upon hearing she was going out with Noah. And she would also likely take credit for her acquiescence.

Despite being excited at the prospect of some adult time without her kids, Andrea was still cautious about whether this connection she had with Noah would lead to anything serious. As Amber said, it was dinner, not a proposal. After making the childcare arrangements, she sent Noah a text letting him know she'd be free for dinner. He responded with an a-okay and thumbs-up emoji.

Setting the phone aside, she hoped and prayed that dating Noah wasn't a big mistake.

Noah made dinner reservations at DiCarlo's, an Italian restaurant in downtown Milwaukee for the following evening. He'd heard from some of the other physicians on staff that it was one of the nicer restaurants in the area. But not so fancy as to be overwhelming on a first date.

The first of many, he hoped.

Truthfully, he'd been surprised Andrea had agreed. Her rule of not dating doctors was rather silly in his opinion, but he supposed that being cheated on had not helped. Especially not knowing about the affair until after her husband had died in a car crash.

A man who would throw away his family was a loser in his book. After meeting Andrea's extended family, all five of her siblings, their spouses, and kids, he found it even more confounding that Stuart would do something like that. Clearly, Andrea's family was held together by love and faith.

Her husband apparently had neither.

Noah paused at his and Josie's wedding photo that he still kept on his dresser. He picked it up, gazing at his wife's face. He missed her, but the deep ache had faded over time. Josie would not want him to stop living his life.

And if he were honest, Josie would have loved Andrea and her family.

He opened the top drawer and tucked the wedding photo away. Josie would always have a piece of his heart, but he no longer grieved his loss as acutely as he had. And the simple truth was that he no longer wanted to live alone.

Andrea had shown him what he was missing.

The following morning, he strode into the surgical intensive care unit early. So much so that none of the day-shift nurses were on the unit yet. The night-shift nurses looked surprised to see him.

He found Jaylon Green, the night-shift resident, in the breakroom in what appeared to be a close intimate conversation with Sonia Allen, one of the night-shift nurses. They were huddled by the scrawny Christmas tree the staff had decorated with unit supplies, strings of gauze as garland and small four by fours made into snowflake ornaments. The moment Noah walked in, Jaylon jumped to his feet as if he were guilty of something. And maybe he was. Noah narrowed his gaze, giving him a pointed look since he knew full well Jaylon was married and that his wife was expecting their first child.

And this, he thought wryly, *is exactly why Andrea had created her rule*. These two had been together all night. He knew as well as anyone that twelve-hour shifts could be long and arduous. It was all too easy to get distracted by a pretty face. At least for some men.

"Oh, you're early," Jaylon said as Noah poured himself some coffee.

"Yep." Noah held his gaze. "How was your night?"

"Not bad." Jaylon moved to the side to give Sonia room to leave. The way their fingers brushed made Noah frown. The worst part, he thought, was that they weren't being at all subtle. "We didn't have to code anyone, which is always good."

Once he and Jaylon were alone, Noah frowned. "What are you doing?" He was purposefully blunt. "You're married and having a baby."

"I'm not doing anything," Jaylon protested, but he averted his gaze in a way that made him look guilty as sin. "We were just talking."

"Don't be an idiot." Even as Noah said the words, he realized his attempt to right a wrong was useless. Men either strayed or they didn't. The sad truth was that even if the senior resident didn't cheat on his wife with Sonia, it seemed that he'd end up finding someone else. Apparently, small things like marriage vows didn't mean anything to the guy.

Why Jaylon had bothered to get married in the first place was a mystery. But it also wasn't his problem. Noah shook off the distasteful thoughts and focused on his day. Since he'd finished the last of the coffee, he set about making a new pot.

As he waited for it to brew, Andrea and a couple of her coworkers came in. She smiled and nodded in greeting.

"Coffee's fresh," he announced, rather unnecessarily.

"Thanks. I'm sure we'll need it." She glanced at her peers, then turned her attention to the census board. "I see a few new patients since yesterday. It didn't take the ED long to fill our empty beds."

"I'll fill you in," Sonia said, returning to the break room. The way she avoided Noah's gaze spoke volumes. There was no doubt in his mind that Jaylon and Sonia had something going on.

Again, not his problem. Noah refilled his coffee mug, then edged past Andrea and Sonia to head into the unit. As the charge nurse, Andrea would be busy. And he needed a formal update about the patients on the unit from his colleagues too.

He'd barely finished reviewing the patients' charts, using the computer on wheels named Mabel, when he heard the triple beep emergency alarm. Abandoning Mabel, he ran down the hall to Mr. Decker's room. He swallowed a groan of frustration when he saw the kid's breathing tube sitting on his chest.

"I don't know how it happened," Kimmy said, frantically trying to use the ambu bag to provide badly needed oxygen to the patient. "I swear, he doesn't even move around much."

"I'll get the intubation cart." Andrea spun and ran back down the hallway to the supply room.

He swallowed a sharp comment, eyeing the monitor above the patient's head. His pulse was already starting to increase to compensate for the lack of oxygen in his blood.

"Let me take over. Please call for the respiratory therapist." Elbowing the nurse aside, he took over providing breaths. His larger hands provided a better seal over Mr.

Decker's nose and mouth, and Noah was relieved to see the patient's oxygen saturation had increased slightly.

Andrea and the respiratory therapist arrived at the same time. Handing the ambu bag to the therapist, he pushed the head of the bed away from the headwall and lowered Decker's head so he could prepare to replace the breathing tube.

He noticed the call light cord was tangled in the oxygen tubing. Gritting his teeth, he realized the knot in the two cords had likely contributed to the patient's breathing tube being accidentally removed.

That was a problem to address later. For now, Noah concentrated on replacing the breathing tube. Andrea handed him the laryngoscope and then held the tube ready for him to place through Mr. Decker's vocal cords.

"He's been intubated for a week," Kimmy said. "It's probably time to consider a trach anyway."

She was right, but that didn't excuse the accidental extubation. He placed the breathing tube, holding it steady while Andrea secured it in place, then connected the patient to the ventilator. When he finished, he looked at Kimmy. "You might be right about Mr. Decker needing a trach, but you also need to keep the tubing from getting tangled up." He gestured to the knot on the bed. "This is how he was extubated. Back in St. Louis, we treated every accidental extubation as a critical event, meaning it should never happen. Central lines being pulled out by accident were treated the same way. I plan to talk to the attendings here about implementing a similar policy."

Kimmy flushed red at his rebuke. "It was an accident."

"No, it was completely preventable," he countered. "But I understand it's not always easy to keep everything straight." He glanced up at the patient's vital signs, relieved to note they were returning to normal. "I've seen patients code and die from something as simple as an unplanned extubation. That's why these events need to be taken seriously."

"I'll help you get things cleaned up," Andrea offered. Noah glanced at her, wondering if she was upset by his comments. She didn't appear to be, but he belatedly realized his approach may have been a slap in the face to the critical care nurses.

As the rest of the day went on, though, Andrea treated him the way she always did, with kindness and respect. When he found her alone in the break room, he tried to apologize.

"I didn't mean to make you and the other nurses angry," he said softly. "But I was being honest about how we viewed unplanned extubations back in St. Louis."

"I'm not angry," Andrea hastily explained. "The truth is that some nurses are just more conscientious than others. I haven't had a self-extubation in a while, but some events like that are more difficult to avoid than others." She grimaced. "Having the tubing knotted up to the point a breathing tube is dislodged is unacceptable in my opinion."

"Thanks." He felt better hearing her say that. "I appreciate your support."

"Of course. It's all about providing the best patient care possible, right?" She smiled, then her portable phone chirped. "Excuse me."

The rest of their twelve-hour shift was relatively uneventful. A far cry from the nonstop emergency situations they'd experienced during the snow emergency. When Andrea's shift was over, she caught his gaze. "I'll see you in a few minutes."

He nodded and quickly changed out of his scrubs and stood in the hallway outside the staff locker room to wait. When she emerged, dressed casually but nicely in a pair of black slacks and a silky red blouse, it was all he could do not to sweep her into his arms for a kiss.

"You look amazing." He gestured toward the elevator. "Ready to go?"

"Yes." She glanced over her shoulder. "I hope nobody sees us leaving together."

Her comment stung, but he did his best to ignore it. As if realizing how that had sounded, she quickly added, "I just think it's better to avoid having our names dragged through the rumor mill."

"I understand." He tucked his hands into his coat pockets. "I made reservations at DiCarlo's. Have you ever been there?"

"No, but I think most of my siblings have all been there." She grinned. "I hear it's great but pricey."

"I don't care about the price as long as the food is good." He was glad she seemed to relax once they left the hospital. He should have considered how it might look for them to start seeing each other. After all, he'd passed judgment on Jaylon and Sonia.

That was related to Jaylon's being married, but still. He steered her toward his Jeep, which was parked a few rows from her vehicle.

He managed some small talk related to her family as they made their way downtown. DiCarlo's had valet parking, so he pulled in and left the car running so he could hand the valet the key fob.

"This looks so nice," Andrea marveled as they headed inside. Before they were shown to their seats, she added, "Thank you for dinner."

"You haven't had anything yet," he protested lightly.

"Doesn't matter. This is amazing already." Her green eyes glowed with happiness.

He tucked his hand in the small of her back as they were led to a private table overlooking the lakeshore. In that moment, he knew he was sunk. Andrea had already captured his heart.

Now he needed to figure out a way to encourage her to give him a chance to prove that most men didn't cheat.

10

———

Andrea couldn't remember the last time she'd eaten dinner at a fancy restaurant like this. The atmosphere at DiCarlo's was amazing. Their table was quiet and private, overlooking the frozen lakeshore.

Being there made her wonder if she was part of the reason Stuart had strayed. Not that his infidelity was her fault, he'd made that decision on his own. But maybe she could have tried harder to have time alone with her husband. To go out on dates more often than once a year on their anniversary.

Granted, Stuart could have tried harder too. Instead of finding someone else to spend time with.

"Hey, what's wrong?" Noah reached across the table to touch her hand. "You look sad."

"Oh, sorry. I'm not." She gave herself a mental shake. Noah deserved her full attention. "I was just thinking that I wish I'd come here sooner."

His dark-brown gaze turned thoughtful. "With your husband."

She flushed. Noah was either really perceptive, or she

was way too easy to read. "I guess. I know his cheating isn't my fault, but I could have done a few things better."

"Nobody is perfect, Andrea." Noah's gaze turned somber. "I had a lot of guilt after Josie was diagnosed. As a doctor, I felt like I should have paid closer attention to her symptoms. That it was somehow my fault that we didn't discover the cancer until it was too late."

"Oh, Noah." She curled her fingers around his. "I'm sure Josie didn't blame you."

"She didn't, but I still wrestled with my guilt just the same." He flashed a wan smile. "Faith helped us get through the devastating diagnosis and Josie's subsequent death. But I was mad at God for a long time afterward."

She nodded slowly. "I was mad at Him too. And like you, I kept thinking I should have known what Stuart was doing before his death."

"We're not mind readers." He tightened his grip on her hand. "We're human; we make mistakes. All we can do is move forward from here."

"I know. It's been easier in a way that Stuart died. At least the kids didn't have to watch us go through a messy divorce."

"That was God's plan for you and your kids." He held her gaze. "And I really hope you realize that Stuart's failures are his alone. No matter what you've been thinking."

She managed to smile. "Thanks, Noah. I didn't mean to get all maudlin." She tugged her hand from his and opened the heavy menu. "Have you eaten here before? What do you recommend?"

Their server must have been watching them because the moment she opened the menu, he approached their table. "Good evening. We have a few specials if you're interested?"

"Very interested," Noah said with a grin.

She smiled back. Noah went with the steak special, and

she chose the grilled salmon. Her kids weren't fans of fish, unless it was of the fish-sticks variety. Which in her mind didn't count.

"What made you decide to go into trauma?" she asked, after their server had taken their orders.

"I liked the idea of putting broken patients back together." He shrugged. "I considered orthopedics, but doing hip and knee replacements seemed too routine and boring. I like the variety of trauma. And I really like taking care of critically ill patients in the ICU."

"I like critical care, too, most of the time. It's not easy when we lose young patients, though." She thought briefly of Mandy Cobb. "I like the variety as well."

"You're an excellent nurse, Andrea." His praise was sweet. "I've noticed how well you chip in to help your colleagues. And I know you've never once had a patient pull out their IV access or their breathing tube while in your care in the six months I've been on duty."

"Thanks." She could feel her cheeks flushing with embarrassment. "I liked what you said about making them never events. Something that shouldn't happen except maybe in rare circumstances."

He nodded, then changed the subject, asking about her kids.

She understood he didn't want their time together to be overly focused on work, but it struck her that it was nice to be able to be able to talk things through with someone who understood. Stuart had never seemed that interested in her job, and after she gave birth to Ben, she'd quit to stay home.

Twelve-hour shifts could be long, and her job required her to work weekends and holidays, case in point, the Christmas Eve snow emergency. But doing something other than being a mom had given her a boost in her confidence, providing a feeling of self-worth. She liked knowing she was helping patients get better.

And she was deeply touched by Noah's praise for her nursing skills.

Her salmon was excellent, and she'd tried a piece of Noah's steak. He'd accepted a bite of her salmon too. By the time their dinner was over, she couldn't believe they'd spent almost two full hours at the restaurant.

"Good thing we're off tomorrow," she said, covering her mouth when she yawned. "We're up way past my bedtime."

"Exactly." He smiled. "Do you have plans for New Year's Eve?"

"No, but I'm working New Year's Day." She shrugged. "It's one holiday the kids won't mind if I miss."

"I get it." If he was disappointed, he didn't show it. The ride back to her house didn't take long. Noah walked her up to the front door, frowning when he eyed her dark house. "Where are the kids?"

"With my sister Amber and her husband, Nick. I'll head over in the morning to pick them up." She unlocked the front door, then looked up at him. "Thanks for dinner, Noah. I had a wonderful time."

"Me too." He held her gaze for a moment, then leaned in for a kiss. It was over before she had a chance to enjoy it, but she was impressed he didn't push for more. "I'll see you at work, Andrea."

"Okay." Her voice sounded breathless.

She flipped on the lights as she made her way to the kitchen. Her lips tingled from Noah's kiss, and she was surprised at how much she'd wanted to wrap her arms around his neck to kiss him back.

Eighteen months was a long time to be alone. And looking back, she'd been alone even before with Stuart's travel schedule. Not that he'd been working as hard as he'd pretended to be.

Enough. There was no point in dwelling on the past. Stuart was gone, and even if he wasn't, they wouldn't be married now anyway. Noah was an amazing man.

Too amazing? As she headed to her room, insidious doubts began to creep in. Noah was tall, dark, handsome, and single. He could have any woman he wanted.

Why her? A widower with two kids?

Was she just an easy mark for him? Did he think she'd fall over herself to date him?

Because she kinda had, she silently admitted.

That night, sleep did not come easily as she wrestled with herself over seeing Noah again.

NOAH WAS in a good mood the following day as he searched for things to do with Andrea and her kids. She had to work New Year's Day, as he did, but they could still do something fun the evening of New Year's Eve.

Ice skating caught his eye, as did a large sledding hill. After a momentary debate, he decided sledding might be better, especially for Ben. Less skill was needed to slide down a hill compared to ice skating.

He was about to call Andrea to see if she was interested when his phone rang. With a frown, he stared at the screen. Why was his colleague Jeff Ramos calling? Reluctantly, he answered. "Hello?"

"Hey, I'm sick," Jeff said, his voice sounding hoarse. "I'm here at work but was hoping you could come relieve me."

Swallowing a groan, Noah sighed. "Sure thing. I'll be there in an hour."

"Thanks." Jeff hacked loudly into the phone before disconnecting.

Noah showered and changed before heading out the door. Jeff Ramos looked rough and sounded worse. Working a shift without Andrea wasn't nearly as fun, but he was soon preoccupied with caring for the critically ill patients.

Mr. Decker was doing better. Mandy Cobb had been transferred to the general floor, and he thought maybe he'd head up to check on her later. There were several new patients that had been brought in overnight; one was a snowplow vs. car. The driver of the car was badly injured with several broken bones, a liver laceration, and a ruptured spleen.

The snowplow will always win out over a car, he thought grimly as he stood at the foot of the patient's bed and entered orders using Mabel. Charles Miller was a thirty-three-year-old man who would be looking at a long road to recovery after this.

The next two hours dragged by slowly. When he heard the overhead announcement about a medical emergency, he grimaced. He knew from Jeff Ramos all the ICUs were full and that they had the only empty bed. That meant no matter what service the floor patient was under, the medical emergency would be transferred down to them as soon as the code team had the situation under control.

He approached Dena, the charge nurse. "We need to move Mrs. Halverson and Mrs. Tibble to the floor."

Dena sighed. "That's going to take some time."

He tried not to show his impatience. "I understand. I'll get the discharge orders written right away. The sooner we free up another bed, the better."

"Okay." Dena looked less than thrilled with the news.

Shaking his head, he knew that if Andrea had been

there, she'd have already been one step ahead of him. He proceeded to enter the discharge orders. Last night when he'd complimented her on being an amazing nurse, she'd brushed it off. Apparently, she didn't realize how much the physicians on duty appreciated having someone like her at the helm. Charge nurses like her made his job ten times easier, especially by being proactive when it came to bed management.

When he'd finished with the orders, he was stunned to realize their new patient was Mandy Cobb. She looked awful, her face pale and lifeless as the floor resident and nurse wheeled her into the unit.

"What happened?" He had thought for sure Mandy's youthful age would work to her advantage.

"She went into full-blown septic shock." The floor resident's expression was grim. Septic shock, a massive infection that raged through the bloodstream, was deadly, regardless of the patient's age. "We believe the source of the infection originated from her amputated fingers and toes."

"Okay, thanks. Let's get IV fluids running wide open." He thought about Decker's case, how his infection had almost taken his life too. "Dena? We need to get Mandy set up with CVVH, stat!"

Dena frowned but didn't protest. Not that arguing would have done her any good. He understood the impact to their staffing, but it couldn't be helped. He needed to do everything possible to save Mandy's life.

"I need the central line cart," he said.

Dena brought it in, then began to set up the continuous venous-venous filtration machine. She did her part, but he still wished Andrea was there.

By the time he'd finished with the catheter, Dena had the machine ready to go. Then she stood at the doorway of the room. "Tammy, can you take over here? I need to make some calls, see if I can get someone to come in to help."

"Yeah, sure." Tammy didn't look up from her task of programming the CVVH machine. "I've got this."

Reassured, Noah moved away to check in on his other patients. It was tempting to text Andrea to let her know Mandy Cobb had bounced back in the unit, but he knew she was spending the day with her kids.

No reason to ruin her day, he thought wryly. Mandy's condition had taken a hard turn for the worse. He knew Andrea would be upset if the young girl they'd cared for during the snow emergency didn't make it. Her compassion and empathy were what made her such a good nurse.

He returned to Mr. Miller's bedside. The guy was fighting the ventilator, so he wrote an order to increase the sedation and for a follow-up CT scan of his abdomen. Noah was worried the guy was bleeding internally. Once the nurse took Charles Miller down to the scanner, he called his attending to mention the possibility of his needing surgery.

"Yeah, okay. We'll need to see what his CT scan shows first, but if the bleeding has increased, we'll put him on the schedule as an urgent case," John Crowley agreed.

"Thanks." Better the patient went to the OR for the exploratory lap than performing the procedure at the bedside. With that situation under control, he headed back down to check on Mandy Cobb. Her pulse was too fast, her breathing shallow, and frankly, he didn't like the way she looked at all.

"We need to get her stabilized. I'd like to put her back on the ventilator. I'll need to insert another breathing tube," he said as Tammy finished with the CVVH machine.

"Okay." Tammy looked flustered but handled the situation well. She darted out of the room to get the intubation cart, then set about assisting with the endotracheal tube placement.

Once he had the breathing tube in place, he stepped back to eye the monitor. The additional support seemed to work, as Mandy's pulse came down a bit, and her breathing was better now that the ventilator was taking over that function.

Now they needed to wait for the antibiotics to kick in. Hopefully sooner rather than later.

He glanced at his watch, realizing it was almost noon. He figured he had just enough time to run down to the cafeteria to grab a sandwich.

"Dr. Weston? There's a call for you on line two," the unit clerk said, before he could leave.

"This is Noah Weston."

"This is Steve Woll, radiologist down in the CT scanner. I thought you should know Charles Miller has a large abdominal hematoma." Dr. Woll paused, then added, "We're estimating another two hundred cc's of blood has oozed into his abdominal cavity. His condition is tenuous, if you ask me."

"I'll be right down." He quickly hung up the phone and glanced around for Dena. There was no sign of her, so he looked at the unit clerk. "Let Dena know I went to radiology. I'm going to get Charles Miller to the OR as quickly as possible."

"Okay." The unit clerk reached for the phone, but he didn't linger. He headed out of the ICU and toward the stairwell that would take him down to radiology. The department was located on the first floor, adjacent to the emergency department.

He found Charles Miller quickly enough. There were two staff members hovering at his bedside. One was Claire, an ICU nurse from the unit, and the other was someone he didn't know, probably a radiology tech.

"His pulse spiked up as we were finishing the scan," Claire said. "I'm worried he's going into shock."

"Run his IVs wide open and increase his O_2 on the ventilator to forty percent." He pulled out his cell phone to call his attending. "John? Charles Miller is actively bleeding into his belly, and his pulse is tachy."

"Okay, sounds like OR suite fourteen is open. I'll meet you there."

"We're heading down to the OR," he told Claire. "Let's get him out of here before he crashes."

Claire nodded and pushed the bed toward the door. The radiology tech helped steer the patient through the hallways to the elevator just outside the department.

Moments later, they were rolling Mr. Miller into OR suite fourteen. His attending, John Crowley, was there, along with an anesthesiologist.

"We'll take it from here," Crowley said with a nod. "I know you need to get back up to the unit."

"Okay. Thanks." He stepped back, wishing he could assist with the procedure. But that wasn't his role today. His job was to medically manage all the patients in the SICU.

Since he was already down in the OR, he decided to detour to the cafeteria on his way back upstairs. His stomach was growling in earnest now.

The line was long, and he tapped his foot impatiently as he waited his turn. The grill line was long, too, but he was in the mood for a grilled chicken sandwich, so he headed over.

"Noah?" Hearing his name, he turned to glance behind him. The female EMT he'd met twice now, Jasmine, smiled as she approached. "It's great to run into you! How are you?"

"I'm good. How are you?" He was surprised to see her.

The EMTs weren't stationed at the hospital, they were off-site at the ambulance substation. He assumed she and her partner had dropped off a patient recently and decided to grab lunch while they were here. He glanced around and didn't see her partner, but maybe he had already gotten something to eat.

"Busy, as usual." She stood close, gazing up at him with interest. It took him a minute to realize she was flirting with him. "I'm so glad I ran into you."

"Oh, well, I don't get out of the ICU very often. My job keeps me busy." His response was lame, but he wasn't sure what else to say. He didn't want to be rude, but he wasn't remotely interested in seeing Jasmine again. The person in front of him moved, bringing him one step closer to being served next. "I'm sure you end up at all the hospitals in the city, right?"

"Yes, but we come here the most." Jasmine put a hand on his arm. "I was hoping we could get together. You know, after work? I'm open tonight or tomorrow. Whatever works best for you."

As he floundered for a nice way to say no, he noticed Andrea had come into the cafeteria. He was so surprised to see her, he froze. What was she doing here? She didn't work today. Then again, he wasn't supposed to be here either.

Her eyes flared with anger as she saw him with Jasmine. Then she abruptly turned and walked away.

"Noah?" Jasmine pressed.

"I'm sorry, I'm not interested. I'm already seeing some-one." He shook off her hand and left the line, intending to catch up with Andrea. But when he glanced around, she was already gone.

11

———

Andrea couldn't believe she'd run into Noah flirting with the pretty EMT they'd met while attending Winter Fest. The EMT, she remembered now, that he'd known by name because he'd met her before. For all she knew, they'd gone out together.

Anger burned hot as she realized he was just like Stuart. Well, that wasn't entirely fair. Obviously, Noah wasn't married or even dating anyone seriously, but still.

She'd thought Noah was interested in her. He'd taken her for a nice dinner and kissed her good-night. She'd let her foolish heart hope that she might find love again.

Yet she knew better. As Amber said, a date wasn't a proposal. Yet she'd really thought . . .

Well, it didn't matter what she'd thought. She was wrong. Better to realize that now than to wait until she was already emotionally invested in him. Noah was a smart, handsome guy who could have anyone he wanted. Including the cute little EMT. There was no reason to think he'd be interested in a single mom with two kids.

Cheeks burning with humiliation, she took the stairs

back up to the SICU. When Dena had called to ask if she'd come in for a few hours, she'd reluctantly agreed. Maggie, Aaron's wife, had asked if the kids could spend the day with their adopted kids, Joey and Max. Andrea had intended to go along to help, but when Dena had called, she'd thought it would be better to make some extra money for her new roof fund. And working a six-hour shift was easier than a full twelve.

She'd intended to grab a quick salad from the cafeteria for lunch. Running into Noah, who wasn't scheduled to work either as far as she knew, had not been part of the plan.

Ducking into the locker room, she quickly shrugged out of her winter coat. She changed her shoes, then slammed the locker door with more force than was necessary. She sighed and tried to calm herself. She was here to take care of patients, nothing more.

Noah probably wished he'd chosen a different day to take the EMT to lunch, she thought darkly. The look of shocked surprise on his features when he saw her would have been comical if it hadn't hurt so much.

Enough. Andrea scrubbed her hands over her face, squared her shoulders, and walked briskly into the ICU. Dena looked harried when Andrea entered the break room. "Oh, Andrea, I'm so glad to see you. Thanks for coming in at the last minute."

"I don't mind helping." Andrea's gaze had gone to the census board. A knot formed in her stomach when she recognized a few names. "Mandy Cobb is back?"

"Yeah, she went into septic shock and is on CVVH. We need her to be a one-to-one patient." Dena eyed her curiously. "You want to take her? I got the impression Tammy isn't as familiar with CVVH patients."

"Yes." Andrea didn't hesitate, even though she knew having one of the sicker patients on the unit meant working closely with Noah. Better that she got used to that, she silently acknowledged. His fellowship was for a full year, which meant he'd be on the unit until June 30 of next year.

Six long months. Oh joy. She sighed and looped her stethoscope around her neck. "I'll get report from Tammy."

"Sounds good," Dena agreed. "Thanks for coming in."

"Sure." She forced a smile, secretly wishing she hadn't come in, but then she decided it was better this way. At least she'd only been foolish enough to go out with Noah once. If she didn't count their time at Winter Fest. Thinking of how well he'd handled her kids brought a lump to the back of her throat. She recalled how the EMT had called Noah by his first name. He'd mentioned they'd met before. She'd thought it was in passing but knew now they'd gotten to know each other along the way.

And if that was the case, why on earth had Noah asked her out? That part didn't make any sense. Especially arranging to spend time with her kids.

Whatever. She gave herself a mental shake and headed out into the unit. She found Tammy staring intently at the CVVH machine with a frown furrowed in her brow. Andrea crossed over to stand beside her. "Hey, Tammy. I'm here to take over Mandy's care."

"I'm glad to hear it." Tammy looked relieved. "I'm not very good with CVVH. I haven't had one in a while. Since I only work part time, it's hard for me to remember how to program the various orders."

"That's okay, I can manage." Andrea only worked part time, too, but she had more years of critical care nursing under her belt. Tammy was only two years out of nursing school. Andrea glanced at Mandy's pale, still face. "She doesn't look good."

"She's not doing well at all. Her parents are on their way in." Tammy grimaced. "Her mother started sobbing on the phone when I updated her."

"I can imagine." Andrea couldn't blame the poor woman. Eloise and Robert Cobb had been crushed by the way Mandy had sneaked out of the house to see her boyfriend on Christmas Eve, only to slide off the road and nearly freeze to death. She and Noah had managed to save her life after the initial hypothermia event, but losing her to sepsis? That seemed so unfair.

Not that anyone promised life would be fair. The fact that she'd lost her husband and that Noah's young wife had died of cancer proved that. The image of Noah smiling and chatting with Jasmine the EMT flashed in her mind. She ruthlessly thrust it aside.

Tammy updated her on the few things she'd done since Mandy had been readmitted to the ICU. Then she left to look in on her other patient.

"Andrea?" Noah's voice came from the doorway. She swallowed hard, glanced at him, then turned her attention back to the CVVH machine. Tammy had entered a few settings wrong, so she quickly fixed them.

"Hey. Dena called me in to help." She nodded at Mandy Cobb. "I was sorry to hear Mandy bounced back from the floor."

"I can explain," he began.

"Don't." The word came out sharply, and she lifted a hand to stop him. "I'm not interested. We need to stay focused on patient care."

"But . . ." His voice trailed off as she avoided his gaze.

"It's almost time for her next dose of antibiotic." The last thing she wanted was to discuss their personal lives, especially while standing at a patient's bedside. Seeing Noah was harder than she'd anticipated. Which was another good reason not to date someone she worked with, she thought sourly. She reviewed the CVVH settings one last time, then moved to edge past him. "Excuse me."

Noah stepped back to give her room. His expression was troubled, and she could feel his gaze boring into her back as she made her way to the medication dispensing machine.

A triple beep alarm rang out. Andrea glanced up at the bank of monitors nearby and noticed a patient on the other end of the hall was experiencing a life-threatening cardiac arrythmia.

As the charge nurse, she'd normally head down to help, but she wasn't in charge today. Dena was. She turned to head back to Mandy's room. The young girl desperately needed her antibiotic.

While the medication infused, she performed a thorough head-to-toe assessment. Mandy's lungs sounded a little wet, as if she had too much fluid swirling in her system. That explained why Noah had ordered the CVVH, to help Mandy handle the fluid load that was needed to combat sepsis.

It was a fine line to walk, keeping the fluids going to help flush out the infection while making sure the girl's kidneys could keep up. This was one of the reasons these patients needed to have only one nurse to manage them. Andrea knew she'd have to keep a close eye on Mandy's condition.

The triple beeping alarm stopped. Since there wasn't a mad rush of staff members heading down to help out, she felt certain the patient's nurse had everything under control.

And that would keep Noah busy too.

Hunger gnawed at her stomach, but she did her best to

ignore it. Once she had Mandy washed up and repositioned, Andrea ducked into the break room to find crackers. There was usually a box of them available for the nursing staff. They would have to do in a pinch.

Noah stepped into the break room, stopping abruptly when he saw her. With her mouth full of crackers, she couldn't say anything.

"Andrea, please let me explain." He looked miserable, but then again, he probably regretted the way she'd found out he was playing the field.

"Noah? I need help in room twelve," a voice called. "He's getting wild again, and I'm worried he'll dislodge his breathing tube!"

He looked frustrated but didn't hesitate to turn, responding to the summons. She watched him go with a sense of regret. She swallowed the crackers, drank a cup of water, then returned to Mandy's room.

Maybe she was being unfair. Maybe he hadn't intended to have lunch with Jasmine. But she couldn't get the image of the two of them standing so close out of her mind.

The simple truth was they'd looked good together. And in her mind, she could understand why he'd be interested in someone like Jasmine rather than her.

Noah did his best to hide his annoyance with the way Andrea was treating him. Why wouldn't she just let him explain? Jasmine had approached him, not the other way around. He'd been caught off guard when she'd asked him out, but he hadn't done anything to warrant Andrea's reaction.

Okay, sure, she'd been burned by her cheating ex. But he

wasn't that kind of guy. And if she couldn't see that for herself, well, then maybe they weren't meant to be.

Cold comfort, he thought as he ordered more sedation for Cole Slatter. The guy's head injury had stabilized, but he was still agitated and combative. When the swelling on his brain went down, he should get better.

At least the patient hadn't hit any other nurses. He still felt bad at how Andrea had been struck by the guy's fist. Thankfully, the bruise around her eye was starting to fade. Today, she hadn't bothered to try to hide it with makeup.

Because she hadn't anticipated seeing him?

No, more likely she hadn't had time. He told himself not to be ridiculous. Andrea was thinking the worst of him based on a brief interaction with another woman.

That was her problem. Not his.

When he finished in Cole Slatter's room, he headed back down the hall to check on his other patients. Mr. Decker was doing so well he entered the order to remove his breathing tube. When that was done, the young man appeared more restful. He stood watching the patient for a moment, making a mental note to consider transferring him the following day if he continued to do well.

He hoped the CVVH therapy would work for Mandy as well as it had for Mr. Decker. Losing young patients was always hard, even if part of the reason they ended up in the SICU was due to their own stupid actions.

Kids would be kids.

That made him think again about Andrea, Bethany, and Ben. He sighed and headed back down the hall to check on Mandy Cobb's condition. When he arrived, the plastic surgery team was at the bedside examining the wounds on her hands and feet from where she'd lost digits due to frostbite.

"Her right hand doesn't look good," the plastic surgeon, a woman by the name of Ginger Ring, said with a frown.

"I agree, that oozing isn't reassuring," Andrea said.

Dr. Ring sighed. "Okay, we'll take her back to the OR for a wound washout and debridement. We were trying to keep as much of her fingers and hand as possible, but I guess we have no choice."

Noah stepped into the room, quickly donning gloves so he could see what they meant. The wound looked nasty, and he wondered if Mandy would lose her entire hand as a result of the raging infection.

"Her parents just got here," Andrea said. "Would you mind giving them an update about your plan?"

"Sure, she's a minor, we need their permission to operate anyway." Dr. Ring covered Mandy's stump with gauze. "Just wrap this loosely, okay?"

"Understood." Andrea made the call down to the family center to get Mandy's parents up to the unit, then wrapped gauze around what was left of the young girl's hand. Noah stepped out to talk to Ginger.

"We have her on CVVH, which obviously can't run while she's in surgery." He tucked his hands into the pockets of his lab coat. "I'd like to discuss her care with the anesthesiologist prior to her going under."

"I understand." Ginger grimaced. "I wish we had another option, but we don't."

"I know." He turned when he heard the double doors to the ICU open. Recognizing Mandy's parents, Eloise and Robert Cobb, he gestured for them to come over. "Mr. and Mrs. Cobb? This is Dr. Ring. She's the plastic surgeon who operated on Mandy's fingers and toes."

"What happened? Why is Mandy back in the ICU?" Rob asked.

"Her right hand wound is infected," Ginger explained. "I'm afraid we'll need to take her back to the operating room to wash out the wound and debride it."

"What does that mean?" Eloise asked. Her red, puffy eyes were full of tears.

"It means we may need to take more of her hand to save her life." Ginger's tone was soft but firm. "I'm sorry, I know this isn't what you want to hear, but it's important, or we wouldn't suggest it. I'll need one of you to sign off on the surgical consent form."

"Oh, Rob." Eloise turned her face into her husband's shoulder.

Robert looked distraught, too, but he nodded. "Of course, we'll sign the consent for surgery. We want Mandy to survive, no matter what."

"Okay, go ahead and see your daughter," Ginger said. "I'll bring in the paperwork as soon as I make the arrangements."

"Thank you." Robert guided his wife into Mandy's room. From the doorway, Noah watched as Andrea greeted them somberly, giving them both a quick hug. He wasn't surprised to see the glint of tears in Andrea's eyes as she spoke to the grieving couple.

She was an excellent nurse.

He turned away to check on the rest of the patients on the unit. Soon he needed to make afternoon rounds. Might as well start reviewing those patients who would be up next to be moved to the floor.

As he walked past a room, he stopped when he noticed Mrs. Tibble was still in the ICU. He'd written her discharge to the floor orders several hours ago. Why was she still there? Scowling at the delay, he strode into the break room to find Dena.

"When is Mrs. Tibble heading out?" he asked bluntly.

"Oh, uh, soon." Dena glanced away, her expression full of guilt. "Her nurse, Tony, wanted to grab lunch first."

That comment made him wonder if Andrea had managed to get anything to eat. He assumed that's why she was in the cafeteria. He shook his head to stop thinking about Andrea. "I would have expected her to be transferred an hour ago. I'd like her moved out ASAP."

"Okay." Dena didn't look him in the eye, as if she knew she'd messed up. "I'll work with Tony to make that happen."

"Please do." He was glad to see Mrs. Halverson had been moved, so they had one empty bed to work with. It was just hard for him to understand why Dena wasn't on top of things. She didn't have any patients to care for. She'd called Andrea in to help, rather than picking up a patient assignment.

His pager app went off on his phone. Seeing the OR was calling, he quickly answered. "This is Noah Weston."

"We're finishing the exploratory lap on Charles Miller," his attending John Crowley said. "We're not going to close him. We've packed his abdomen with gauze so we can do a staged abdominal repair on him over the next few days. We'll send him back up to the SICU in ten to fifteen minutes."

"Thanks. I'll update the nursing staff." Noah ended the call and went out to find Dena, surprised to find her packing Mrs. Tibble's belongings. "Charles Miller will be up in ten to fifteen minutes. His belly will remain packed as they plan on taking him to the OR again either tomorrow or the next day."

"Okay, thanks." Her cheeks flushed red as if she realized her mistake in not getting the patient out sooner. "I'll let Claire know."

"Thanks." He turned away, grabbed Mabel the COW, and headed toward Charles Miller's room. Once the patient arrived back from the OR, he'd need to complete a whole new set of orders. Might as well get started on them now.

A few minutes later, Claire came into the room and began double-checking the supplies. Mr. Miller arrived shortly thereafter, and soon, they were both busy with the new arrival.

When the orders were finished, and Mr. Miller was settled in, Noah went back out to start afternoon rounds. The process took longer than usual. By the time he'd finished, his shift was just about over.

Andrea's, too, he noticed as she stood at Mandy Cobb's bedside giving report to the night-shift nurse Sonia. The same one he'd seen cozied up to his resident Jaylon Green.

When he'd finished updating Jaylon, Noah headed into the breakroom. There was no sign of Andrea, so he checked the locker room.

The door was closed, so he didn't go inside. Instead, he stood out in the hallway, waiting. When Andrea emerged a few minutes later, she frowned when she saw him.

"I'm not interested in Jasmine," he said. "She found me in the cafeteria, not the other way around."

Andrea shrugged. "You have a right to date anyone you like."

He bit back a flash of anger. She acted as if they were strangers. "I'm only interested in you, Andrea. No one else."

She sighed and stared down at her booted feet for a long second. "Why?"

"Why am I interested in you?" He frowned. "Because you're smart, beautiful, and an amazing mother to your kids."

"You don't really want to be saddled with anyone else's kids."

She was really starting to make him mad. "Andrea, I care about you. We've gotten close over the past few months. Or so I thought. We connected during the snow emergency, too, or so I thought. Are you telling me you're not interested in me?"

She grimaced. "I'm not sure I'm ready for a relationship. I don't want to expose my kids to someone who isn't interested in the long haul."

"Why would you assume I'm not interested in the long haul?" He was starting to get mad again. "Come on, Andrea. You saw me talking to Jasmine. I'm sorry you thought it was more than a chance meeting. I never cheated on my wife or on any of my girlfriends. That's not who I am."

She looked uncertain for a moment, then took a step toward the elevator. "I think it's best if we just stay friends, Noah."

"Friends," he repeated duly. She took another step toward the elevator. "Is that really what you want?"

"Yes." She lifted her chin. "I think that's for the best. Have a good evening." With that, Andrea turned and hurried away. She was in the elevator, the door closing behind her before he could move.

Not that there was any point to chasing her. Andrea had made her stance perfectly clear.

She wasn't interested. As much as it hurt to realize his feelings for her were one-sided, there was nothing he could do. Andrea had her own issues to work out.

He'd planned to apply for an attending position here at Trinity Medical Center, but maybe he was better off heading back to St. Louis once his fellowship was over.

12

———

Andrea's stomach rolled queasily as she drove to her brother Aaron's home in Brookland. She wanted to believe it was related to not eating lunch or dinner, but she knew it wasn't.

Noah's wounded expression haunted her. He hadn't taken Jasmine to lunch, the way she'd assumed. That she'd gotten a glimpse of him with another woman and acted as if he were like her deceased husband wasn't right.

She should have apologized to him. Instead, she'd pushed him even farther away.

After pulling into Aaron and Maggie's driveway, she rested her forehead on the steering wheel for a moment. There was no sense in crying over the way she'd left Noah standing outside the locker room. It was done.

And it was probably for the best.

Yet if that was the case, why did she feel so sick?

Pushing out of the car, she hurried up to the front door. Maggie answered instantly, carrying the now three-year-old Max on her hip. "Hey, you're just in time for pizza if you're hungry."

"I could eat," Andrea said, even though she wasn't hungry. "Thanks. How were the kids?"

"Great. Joey and Ben had fun playing. Bethany helped me with Max." Maggie cocked her head to the side. "How was work? Looks like you had a rough day."

"It was fine." The rough part was walking away from Noah, but she didn't mention it. "Is Aaron around?"

"No, he was called in to Children's Memorial for an urgent pediatric heart case." Maggie bent to set Max down on the floor. The three-year-old ran across the room and promptly tripped over his own feet. When he started to cry, Bethany hurried over.

"Hey, it's okay, Max." Her daughter lifted the little boy to his feet. "Let's play with your building blocks."

"See?" Maggie closed the door behind Andrea. "She's a natural."

"Yeah, she's great with the younger kids as long as they're not her brother." She followed her sister-in-law into the kitchen. There was leftover pizza on the table, so she helped herself, hoping the food would quell the nausea. "Maggie, do you mind if I ask you a question?"

"Go ahead." Maggie waved at the fridge. "You want something to drink?"

"No thanks, I'm fine." She nibbled the cheese and pepperoni pizza. "Did you date other guys while you and Aaron were divorced?"

Maggie dropped into the chair beside her. "I tried to date other men, but honestly, I wasn't at all interested." She shrugged. "Despite everything Aaron and I had been through, I still cared for him. No, the truth was I still loved him. And that made it impossible for me to move on."

Andrea had heard something similar from Aaron, how their divorce had not changed his feelings for Maggie either.

She thought it was sweet that they were destined to be together. "And now you're married again."

"Yes." Maggie laughed and ate a piece of pepperoni. "I think God had a plan for us, and we were just too stubborn to go along with it until we were forced together again."

Andrea stared down at her half-eaten slice of pizza. "How did you know Aaron was the right one? I mean, I thought Stuart was great until I discovered he was cheating on me."

"Stuart's cheating is his failure, not yours." Maggie reached over to take her hand. "I wish you didn't have to suffer that experience, Andrea. I can only imagine how betrayed you felt. But honestly, I never once doubted Aaron's love. Not in that way. I never once thought he'd cheat." She smiled. "He's too much like your father."

Andrea managed to smile back. "That is one thing about the Monroe men. They're dedicated to their spouses."

"Absolutely. You can just tell with some men, the way they only have eyes for the woman in their life. It's the way Alec looks at Jillian, the way Adam looks at Krista, and Austin looks at Lindsey. Even the way Nick looks at Amber. It took me a while to accept that Aaron was the same way with me."

"You're right. I guess I should have paid closer attention to that when I started dating Stuart."

"Don't blame yourself." Maggie's tone was sharp. Then her expression softened. "Is this about Noah? He seems like a great guy."

Andrea sighed and pushed her half-eaten pizza away. "Yes. I just told him I wasn't interested in seeing him again."

"Why?" Maggie looked puzzled. "The man couldn't keep his eyes off you at Christmas."

She closed her eyes and groaned. "I saw him in the cafeteria chatting with a pretty EMT and immediately thought the worst."

"Oh, Andrea." Maggie reached over to pat her shoulder. "I can see why your initial instinct was to jump to conclusions, but you must know that's not Noah's style. From what I've heard, he was a dedicated husband to his wife while she suffered from cancer."

"He was dedicated to her. All the way up to the end." And that, Andrea realized was a key component to Noah's true character. Would Stuart have been there for her if she'd been diagnosed with some fatal illness? He had rarely been home as it was, and she couldn't see him taking care of her. Or the kids for that matter.

Now that she thought about it, there were lots of times she'd been upset with Stuart for his lack of caring about their family. He'd always assured her things were fine, but they weren't. And that was partially her fault too. "I ignored the warning signs with Stuart." She met Maggie's gaze. "Deep down, I knew something was off between us, but I didn't push him for more."

"Again, his cheating is not your fault," Maggie pointed out. "Stop thinking it's about you when it's totally about him."

"Okay, I can accept that, but it's still hard to understand what Noah sees in me." She turned to look at the kids in the playroom. "A mother with two kids? Why on earth would he be interested in us?"

"You act as if love is logical." Maggie shook her head. "It's not. Don't you think I tried to fall out of love with Aaron during our divorce? I did. I told myself he wasn't worth it. That he'd moved on, so I should too. I tried to date other men, but they left me cold. It took me a year to realize I would always love your brother. That nobody else could replace him in my heart." She reached over to touch Andrea's hand. "It's time for you to stop looking for logic and to start following your heart."

"My heart belongs to Noah." The words popped out of her mouth before she could stop them.

"I know that, and if you ask me, Noah's heart belongs to you too." Maggie pushed her half-eaten pizza back toward her. "Finish your dinner. I think we'll keep the kids overnight so you and Noah can talk."

It was a sweet offer, but Andrea shook her head. "There's no need for you to do that. It's too late for me to make up with Noah. I already told him I wasn't interested."

"It's never too late." Maggie grinned. "Aaron and I are the perfect example. It took losing Joey's mother in a car crash and my determination to adopt him to bring us back together. And that was after being divorced for a couple of years." Her sister-in-law's expression softened. "Look at how far we've come since then, Andrea. We have Joey and Max, two amazing kids, and I can honestly say we've never been happier. Trust me, Andrea, you need to let go of your pride and your ego and listen to your heart. The way Aaron and I finally did."

"I'm glad it worked out for you two. Because we always knew you were perfect for each other." Andrea forced herself to finish the pizza. Was Maggie right? Could she salvage things with Noah?

The only way to know was to try.

She pulled out her phone and stared at the screen. Then she scrolled through her recent contacts to find Noah's number. Still, she couldn't bring herself to call him.

Text? No, too impersonal.

"Go on, call him." Maggie rose to her feet. "I'll give you some privacy."

What she needed was courage. When Maggie left her alone in the kitchen, Andrea drew in a deep breath and made the call. To her surprise, Noah answered on the first ring, his voice etched with concern. "Andrea? Are you okay? The kids? Is something wrong?"

"Nothing is wrong. The kids are fine. But I wanted you to know I'm sorry for the way I acted today. You didn't deserve my anger or jealousy." There was a moment of silence on his end, so she pressed on. "I don't know why I overreacted. I guess the truth is that I can't understand why you're even interested in me. It was easier for me to believe you would rather be with Jasmine."

"Andrea, I understand your husband's actions eroded your self-confidence, but trust me, you're a very attractive woman. More so than Jasmine."

Her cheeks flushed hot, and she was glad they weren't on a video call. "I don't know about that."

He sighed loudly enough that she could hear. "I do. Where are you? At home?"

"Um, no, I'm at my brother's house in Brookland. Why?"

"I'm coming over. What's the address?"

Startled, she told him.

"Great. See you in a few minutes." He ended the call before she could say anything more.

And just like that, Noah was rushing to her side. Something Stuart had never done. Or at least, not in the last few years of their marriage.

Suddenly ravenous, she quickly ate another piece of pizza. Maggie came back into the room. "Well?"

"Noah's coming over." She gestured to the leftover pizza. "Do you mind if he has some pizza too?"

"Of course not. Help yourselves." Maggie's smile lit up her entire face. "See, I told you it wasn't too late."

"Yeah, you did." She was still nervous about seeing Noah. It was hard to admit how stupid she'd been to overreact. To assume there was more behind their chance meeting that there was.

And yet she still had trouble understanding why on earth he was interested in someone like her.

NOAH HAD to force himself to drive the speed limit on his way to Aaron Monroe's home in Brookland. When he saw Andrea's car in the driveway, he relaxed. Part of him had worried she would leave before he had a chance to get there.

Andrea opened the door when he knocked, offering a hesitant smile. "Hi, Noah."

"Hey. Thanks for waiting." He stepped across the threshold, glancing around with interest. "Wow, this is very nice."

"Thank you." Maggie took his coat. "Why don't you and Andrea go into the kitchen? We have leftover pizza if you're hungry."

"Great, I'm starving. I didn't get lunch." He glanced at Andrea, then added, "Leftover pizza is perfect, thanks."

Andrea led the way into a kitchen that was almost the size of his condo's living room. "I can heat a plate for you in the microwave."

"No need." Despite being hungry, he caught her hand in his. "Let's talk first."

"Okay." She looked up at him. "I really am sorry I treated you badly."

He was glad she'd apologized. "That's okay. I just want you to know that I didn't seek her out in any way. She asked me out, not the other way around."

"I can understand why she'd be interested in you."

Andrea's brow furrowed. "It's why you're interested in me that I don't get."

He shook his head. "That's your lack of self-confidence talking. Come on, Andrea, be honest. Are you seriously telling me none of the doctors on staff have ever asked you out?"

"They have, but I never took their interest seriously." She tucked a strand of her dark hair behind her ear.

"That's because you have a dim view of dating doctors." He searched her gaze. "Right? I heard all about that when I first started back on July first. The truth is you're very attractive. Trust me, I'm not the only one who thinks so."

She started to protest, then caught herself. "I have two kids. That alone puts some men off."

He wanted to shake some sense into her. "Some men, maybe. But not anyone who is interested in settling down. Like me."

She looked up at him in surprise. "Really?"

"Really. And it's more than your looks." He struggled to find a way to explain. "It's all of you. The whole package." At her skeptical glance, he waved a hand. "Why is this so hard for you to understand? You're an amazing person on the inside, Andrea. Not only do you manage the ICU better than anyone else, but you're a great mother to your kids. The compassion you give to your patients and families comes from your heart. And seeing you with your siblings only made me like you more."

"Most nurses care about their patients," she said.

He tried not to sigh. "Like I said, it's the whole package. I was attracted to you from the very beginning, but those feelings only grew more intense as we worked together over time." He reached out to snag her other hand, pulling her closer. "You're the one I gravitated to. The one I couldn't stop watching. The one I wanted to work with every shift if I could. Nobody else. Just you."

Her jaw dropped as she looked up at him. "Oh, Noah. I don't know what to say."

"Maybe that you feel the same way?" He offered a crooked smile. "That you noticed me too?"

"I did. I do." The simple admission shot straight to the center of his heart. "I fought against my feelings for you because . . . well, you know." She flushed. "I realize you're nothing like Stuart. I guess you're right about my self-confidence taking a hit. I keep wondering why Stuart found someone else."

"Because he's an idiot that didn't know a good thing when he had it." Noah drew her closer. "The truth is you're everything I've wanted in a woman."

"I'm going to try really hard to believe you on that," she murmured wryly.

He lowered his head to kiss her. She instantly melted into his arms, encouraging him to deepen the kiss. Heat flared hot between them, and he had to remind himself they were standing in the middle of her brother's kitchen, with her kids playing in the other room.

"Wow," Andrea whispered, when he ended the kiss. Her dazed expression warmed his heart. "That was amazing."

He grinned. "It was. Because we were meant to be together."

She laughed, blushing at that. "As much as I tend to agree, I still have the kids to worry about." Her expression turned serious. "I want to continue seeing you, Noah, but we might need to take things slow. So the kids can get used to the idea."

Slow just might kill him, but he kept his thoughts to himself. Part of the reason he liked her so much was the way she put her kids first. "We can take things as slow as you'd like. I'm in this for the long term, Andrea. There's nothing I want more than for your kids to approve of us being together."

"I don't think it will take them too long to get used to it. They don't miss their father nearly as much as I thought they would," she said in a low voice. "In hindsight, I can see how Stuart kept them at arm's length. Oh, he was the fun dad when he was home, but he wasn't there when they needed him. I'm sure that was because he'd already planned on filing for divorce."

Again, if Stuart wasn't dead, Noah would be tempted to punch him in the face. But of course, he didn't voice that thought either. Stuart was gone, and in his opinion, that was good riddance. He wanted Andrea to realize she was worth far more than the way the guy had treated her. But it would take some time, he knew, for her to get some of her self-confidence back. Sooner or later, she'd realize how much he liked and admired her. "We can start by going sledding on New Year's Eve. I'm sure they'll have a blast. I won't keep you out too late, as we are both scheduled to work the next day."

"They will have a great time. And so will I," she added. "It's a date. I can make dinner for us, too, if you'd like. Nothing too fancy," she warned. "Maybe a Crock-Pot beef stew that can cook while we're sledding."

"That sounds great." He bent his head to kiss her again. "I promise you won't regret this."

"Andrea? Oh, sorry." He straightened and glanced over his shoulder to see Maggie Monroe standing behind them, grinning widely. There was no doubt she'd seen the kiss and heartily approved. "Bethany wants to know if they can stay overnight. Ben and Joey would like more time to play as well."

"Oh, I don't think that's necessary," Andrea said, then stopped abruptly to look at him, her gaze uncertain. "Unless you'd like to grab something to eat? I mean, something other than leftover pizza?"

"I'd love that." He could have kissed Maggie for offering to keep the kids. He was convinced she'd overheard at least part of their conversation and was doing her part to push them together. Granted, he'd agreed to take things slow, but this could officially be their second date. "Thanks, Maggie."

"Anytime." Maggie waved them off. "Go, have fun."

Noah grabbed his coat from the sofa, then found Andrea's too. He held it out for her, then escorted her outside. She stopped for a moment to look up at the starry sky.

"What is it?" he asked, following her gaze.

"I'm just thanking God for bringing you into my life." She turned to smile at him.

"Andrea." He pulled her in for another kiss. "It's not going to be easy to take things slow if you keep saying stuff like that."

She laughed. "We'll see how it goes."

He hugged her close, thinking that no matter how long he had to wait for her to be ready for more, it would be worth it.

He wasn't going anywhere without her.

EPILOGUE

Valentine's Day . . .

Andrea knew Noah had made reservations for DiCarlo's again, the same place they'd gone on their first date. She had learned he'd applied for the open trauma attending physician position and wondered if he had good news to share.

They'd seen each other as often as possible over the past six weeks. Their schedules didn't always mesh, and she had the kids' activities to deal with too. Noah never minded, and the times they were alone together were extra special.

Tonight, her kids were spending the night with Alec and Jillian and their daughter, Shannon. She felt guilty for that, but Alec had reminded her of how often she'd watched Shannon when he'd been a single father.

"Family helps family," Alec had said firmly. "Besides your kids help keep Shannon occupied too. Win-win, right?"

"Thanks, Alec." She knew there was no reason to feel bad. Bethany and Ben loved spending time with their cousins.

At five minutes to six, Noah knocked at her door. She smiled up at him, tempted to pinch herself, as he looked as amazing as always. "Hi."

"Hi yourself." He grinned and pulled her in for a kiss. "Ready to go?"

"Yep." She shrugged into her coat and followed him outside. The cold February wind was brutal, but she barely noticed. "Happy Valentine's Day, Noah."

"Same to you." His smile warmed her heart.

"How was work?" She knew he'd filled in for a few hours. The night-shift resident had agreed to come in early so they could still have dinner.

"Fine." He shrugged and glanced at her. "The unit never runs as smoothly when you're not there."

She rolled her eyes. "Flattery will get you nowhere."

"Okay, I will tell you that Mandy Cobb came back to visit the staff." He reached for her hand. "She was in a wheelchair that she was able to propel herself. She seems to be hanging in there, despite losing both her hands and feet."

"That poor girl," Andrea said with a sigh. "She's really been through a lot."

"Yeah. The good news is that she's being fitted for her bilateral foot prosthesis. Once she's up and walking, they'll fit her for two hands as well. She's young. I think she'll learn to adapt without a problem."

"I hope you're right." She glanced at Noah. "I don't think any of the doctors on the unit care about their patients as much as you do."

"Flattery will get you whatever you like," he teased.

She laughed. When they reached the restaurant, she was surprised to see they had been given the exact same table. "Did you ask for this on purpose?" she asked, as Noah pulled her chair out for her.

"Yep." He didn't immediately take his seat. Instead, he went down on one knee and held out an engagement ring. "Andrea, I love you. Will you please marry me?"

"Noah." She stared at the engagement ring, then remembered what Maggie said about love having nothing to do with logic. She smiled. "I love you too. And I'd like nothing more than to marry you."

His face bloomed in a wide smile as he stood and pulled her to her feet. He kissed her as the patrons in the restaurant clapped.

She kissed him back, then blushed at the attention. Noah slid the engagement ring onto her finger, then said, "Your father made me promise to never hurt you the way Stuart did. I want you to know I will always love and cherish you and the kids."

"I know you will." She kissed him again. "Because you're a man just like my father. And I can't wait to be your wife."

"Does that mean we're not taking things slow anymore?" he asked hopefully. "I was given the attending physician job, by the way, so it's too late for you to back out now."

She laughed again. "Don't worry, I don't think we need to have a long engagement."

"Good." His dark eyes gleamed with anticipation. "That gives me time to convince you to have another baby."

A baby? She nodded slowly. "I'd like that. Very much."

"Good. We can start thinking of more B names. I like Brandon for a boy and Bella for a girl. What do you think?"

"I think we should get married first." She couldn't help but laugh. "Then talk about names for our future kids."

His gaze clung to hers for a long moment. "I love you, Andrea."

"I love you too." As they sat down to eat, she looked

outside at the lakefront and, once again, thanked God for bringing Noah Weston into her life.

I hope you enjoyed reading about the Monroe family! If you're interested in more of my books, I'm kicking off a new series next year. The first book in my Grayson's Guardians series is *Deadly Abduction*. If you'd like to check it out, click here!

DEAR READER

Thanks for reading *White Christmas*! I hope you enjoyed Andrea and Noah's story. I've had fun writing about the Monroe siblings. While I'm sad the series has come to an end, I'm already working on my next series! The first book in my Grayson's Guardians Series, *Deadly Abduction*, will be available early next year! I never formally introduced you to Joel Sullivan's high school friend Grady McFarland, but you'll meet him soon enough. I hope you give my new series a try.

Don't forget, you can purchase ebooks or audiobooks directly from my website and will receive a 15% discount by using the code **LauraScott15**.

I adore hearing from my readers! I can be found through my website at https://www.laurascottbooks.com, via Facebook at https://www.facebook.com/LauraScottBooks, Instagram at https://www.instagram.com/laurascottbooks/, and Twitter https://twitter.com/laurascottbooks. Please take a moment to subscribe to my YouTube channel at youtube.-com/@LauraScottBooks-wr1xl?sub_confirmation=1. Also take a moment to sign up for my monthly newsletter to learn about my new book releases! All subscribers receive a free novella not available for purchase on any platform.

Until next time,

Laura Scott

PS. Keep reading for a sneak peak of *Deadly Abduction*...

DEADLY ABDUCTION

Chapter One

Grady "Mac" McFarland stared at his boss, Rex Grayson. Normally, he gave his former Army Captain a lot of respect, but Rex seemed to have gone off the deep end this time. This mission was unlike any of the others Grayson's Guardians had sent him on. To the point he wasn't sure he'd heard him correctly. "You really want me to be a bodyguard for a rich woman and her seven-year-old kid?"

Rex nodded. The captain was only four years older than Grady's thirty-two, but the grim weariness in his boss's gray eyes betrayed the emotional toil they'd suffered during their last tour in Iraq. Grady—he was only Mac to his Army buddies—knew that Rex had taken the loss of their teammates hard, and that he'd ended up getting divorced after he'd returned stateside. From what Grady could tell, his boss was still grieving. "Yeah, that's exactly what Ms. Lauren Chandler is asking and paying us for. I really need you to do this."

"Why me?" The question popped out before he could stop it. The truth was, someone from the team had to take this assignment. Granted, they were usually sent on rescue or recovery missions. None of them were experts on keeping an eye on a socialite and her daughter.

"Because you have good instincts and even better investigative skills." When his phone dinged, Rex reached for it. "Ms. Chandler has some strong opinions on who she'll accept as her bodyguard. Besides, I have a feeling that we're going to need to work with the police and the FBI on this." Rex held up his phone. "She's here."

Grady swallowed a groan as he rose to his feet. The door to the office swung open revealing a stunning blonde wearing a long leather coat that probably cost more than his house back in Cody Wyoming. Lauren Chandler looked rich, even without the sparkly diamond studs in her ears and the expensive looking clothes. She had a large leather handbag that matched her coat, slung over her shoulder. She looked to be roughly his age, he thought. Her pale skin indicated she didn't get out in the sun much, or maybe it was just that it was early February in Chicago. The young girl beside her had long brown hair that was held back from her face with a pink headband, and the same brilliant blue eyes as her mother. The little girl also wore a thick navy-blue parka in deference to the freezing cold Chicago temperatures.

Not unlike Wyoming, he thought with a sigh. No such luck he'd be sent to Florida or some other southern state in the winter.

"Ms. Chandler this is Mac, er Grady McFarland. Mac, this is Ms. Lauren Chandler and her daughter Lucy."

"Nice to meet you." He forced a smile on his face as he

stepped forward to offer his hand. To his surprise, Lauren shook it with a firm grip.

"Thanks for agreeing to help me." She glanced at her daughter, and amended, "Help us."

"I was just about to fill Mac in on what's been happening." Rex gestured to the chairs beside his. "Please have a seat."

Lauren removed her leather bag and dropped gracefully into the chair beside his. Her daughter took the seat on her other side almost as if Lauren had purposefully put herself between him and Lucy. He frowned, not appreciating being viewed as a threat to the little girl.

"A seven-year-old girl was abducted two days ago," Rex said, breaking the silence. "Her name is Ariel Turner and she happens to be one of Lucy's closest friends. They attend the same private school together."

Grady frowned. "And Ms. Chandler believes that abduction is an indication Lucy is also in danger?" To his mind that was a leap, even if Lucy's parents were rich.

"Please, call me Lauren. I have video on my laptop." She surprised him by removing a computer from her large bag and opening it. "I think when you see this, you'll understand my concern."

Rex inclined his head, indicating she should go ahead with the video. Grady leaned over to see the screen as Lauren queued up the video. A whiff of her perfume teased his senses, but he ignored it. As a client, Lauren was off limits, even if she wasn't rich and had a daughter. *Three strikes you're out,* he thought wryly. Besides, he wasn't interested in dating anyone after his former fiancée broke things off. His job caused him to travel across the US, and frankly he liked the different missions Rex Grayson assigned to them. *Until this most recent request,* he silently amended.

Beside him, Lauren expanded the video on the screen and hit the play button. A young girl wearing a navy-blue parka and a pink headband walked down the sidewalk. She wore white tights beneath a navy blue and green plaid pleated skirt. At first, he thought the girl was Lucy, as they both had brown hair and the same pink headband, but as he searched the girl's facial features, he realized it wasn't.

A man wearing a ski mask suddenly appeared in the screen. He swooped the girl into his arms, covering her mouth with his hand as he darted away. The kidnapping happened so fast, Mac blinked in surprise when the short video ended.

"What in the world?" He glanced at Lauren. "Do the police have any leads on who did this? Is there more video that shows the vehicle the kidnapper used to escape?"

"No." Her expression was strained. "The most interesting thing is that Ariel was released less than three hours later." She paused, then added, "After the kidnappers realized they'd grabbed the wrong girl."

A chill snaked down his spine. Okay, now he understood. He caught a glimpse of Lucy's concerned face and framed his comment as carefully as possible. "You believe your daughter is in danger."

Lauren's blue eyes flashed. "I know she is."

"Ariel was scared." Lucy's voice was small. "But the bad man didn't hurt her."

Mac's throat tightened at the thought of Lucy being snatched the same way Ariel had been. He sat up straighter, absorbing the gravity of the situation. "Do Ariel and Lucy always dress alike? I mean, other than wearing their school uniform."

Lauren nodded. "They like to pretend to be twins." Her brow furrowed. "Although not anymore."

"Ariel's mother doesn't like me." Lucy's blue eyes were bright with tears. "She said we can't play together anymore."

"It's okay, Lucy." Lauren wrapped her arm around her daughter's slim shoulders, hugging her close. "Ms. Turner is just upset about what happened. I'm sure that once the bad man is behind bars everything will go back to normal."

"I hope so." Lucy's voice was muffled against her mother's coat. "Ariel is my best friend."

"I know, sweetie." Lauren's stricken gaze turned to Mac's. "Lucy needs protection. And We also need to understand the source of the threat."

Grady glanced at Rex, then slowly nodded. "I'm sure the local police and the FBI are working on that as well."

"They are, but not with the sense of urgency I expect." Lauren's blue eyes glittered with anger. "Ariel being released has lulled them into complacency. They aren't taking the threat as seriously as I'd like."

He arched a brow at that. When Rex didn't say anything, he nodded. "Okay, let's start with who might have a grudge against you."

Lauren glanced at Lucy, then back at him. "I'd be happy to discuss this at length when we get home."

Grady almost argued, but then realized Lauren didn't want to go into details in front of her daughter. With a resigned sigh, he nodded. "Fine. What's your address? I can meet you there."

She arched a brow. "I'm not leaving without you. My driver dropped us off and escorted us up to the tenth floor. From here, I expect you'll be handling all aspects of our transportation."

She expected him to be her chauffer? Great. He did his best to hide his annoyance. "I'm driving a Jeep, not a limo."

"I didn't expect a limo." Her tone held a note of disdain. "And there's one more thing we need to discuss."

He glanced again at Rex, who grimaced as if he knew what was coming. He braced himself for the worst. Did she expect him to wear some sort of chauffer's uniform? Or some other uniform to make sure he blended into the background when she did—whatever rich socialites did.

"I need you to pretend to be my fiancé." Lauren turned to face him. "I don't want the world to know my daughter is in danger."

He blinked. That was so not what he'd expected. "Your fiancé."

"Yes." A faint blush stained her cheeks. "From what I understand you're not involved with anyone, correct?" When he managed to nod in agreement, she went on, "Then there's no reason the public in general won't buy our story."

"Except for the fact we've only seen each other for the first time today," he drawled. Or the fact that he was a former Army sergeant from Cody Wyoming, about as far from the high society page as you could get.

Annoyance flashed in her eyes as she glanced toward Rex. His boss cleared his throat. "Mac, er, Grady will gladly take on the role of your fiancé to keep you and your daughter safe."

He would? Swallowing a flash of irritation, he forced a nod. "Of course. Whatever you think is best."

"Thank you." Satisfied with the arrangement, Lauren rose. She dug a check from her handbag which doubled as a computer case and set it on Rex's desk. "For the first week as agreed. I'm hoping you, Grady and the police are able to figure out who is responsible for abducting Ariel by then."

"Thank you." Rex glanced at the check then rose. He

held out his hand. "Mac, er Grady will protect you and your daughter with his life."

"I'm counting on it." Lauren's expression was grim as she shook Rex's hand, then turned to him. "Would you like to be called Grady or Mac?"

He cleared his throat. "Grady is fine. It's only my Army buddies that call me Mac."

"Fine." She nodded briskly. "Let's go then." She placed her computer in her bag and was about to sling it over her shoulder when he held out his hand. It took a moment for her to realize he intended to carry it for her. "It looks like a purse," she said, clearly flustered by his action.

"That's okay." He didn't care what it looked like, he wasn't about to let her carry it. He shrugged into his leather bomber jacket and took the bag from her hand. "I've got it."

"Thank you." She turned to her daughter. "Let's go, Lucy."

As he followed Lauren and Lucy out of the office he turned to shoot one last look at Rex. He wasn't the only single agent Rex had working for him. They were all single, although Brody was seeing someone last Grady had heard.

The only reason he was going along with this pretend fiancé bodyguard deal was the video of the masked man snatching Ariel off the street in broad daylight and knowing Lucy was the intended target.

Rex was right about one thing. He'd protect Lucy and her mother with his life if necessary. Although he grimly hoped it wouldn't come to that.

∽

LAUREN GLANCED FURTIVELY over her shoulder as she stepped out of the office building into the bright sunshine.

Her face felt like it might crack from her forced smile. Every nerve ending was on high alert, waiting for the masked man to pop out of the shadows at any moment.

She hadn't slept in the two days since Ariel had been abducted by mistake. And even with hiring a bodyguard, she couldn't relax. One man could only do so much. She'd been tempted to ask for an entire team of bodyguards, but that would only advertise the danger.

"Stay a few feet in front of me." Grady's low husky voice had her glancing at him. Then she just as quickly looked away. He was tall, broad shouldered and incredibly handsome if you liked rugged looking men with hair that was too long and needed to be cut.

Which to her dismay, her long-dormant hormones did.

Grady put his arm around her waist, keeping her positioned to his left. She kept Lucy close, then stiffened when she realized Grady held a gun in his right hand.

Well, what did you think? She mentally chided herself. Of course her bodyguard would be armed with a weapon.

"You're supposed to be my fiancé," she whispered as he directed her to his car. He'd said he drove a Jeep, but somehow she'd expected something with a rag top that he'd use to go four wheeling in the mountains, not a brand new Jeep Grand Wagoneer. It was an expensive looking car. Something she wouldn't mind driving.

"Yeah, but this fiancé plans to be ready for anything." He hustled her to the passenger side door. "Does Lucy need a booster seat?"

"Technically, yes, but for now she'll be fine." The booster seat was the least of her worries, although she was a little surprised he'd mentioned it. Most single guys were clueless about that kind of thing. Unless, Grady had kids? Whatever. It didn't matter, as long as he did his job.

Except it did matter if he was going to put his life on the line for her. She waited for Lucy to get settled in the back seat, before climbing in herself. When Grady slid behind the wheel, she asked, "Do you have kids?"

"What? No." He looked startled by her question. "Why do you ask?"

"I—was surprised you knew about booster seats."

"I may have grown up in small town Wyoming, but I didn't live under a rock." His western drawl was back. "I'm friends with a guy who has eight siblings. I'm familiar with what it's like to be around kids."

"I see." She flushed. "I didn't mean any disrespect."

"None taken." He said the words easily, but she sensed his annoyance. She closed her eyes and tried to calm her racing heart. There was no reason to care what Grady McFarland thought about her. He was her bodyguard and fake fiancé. Once this nightmare was over, she'd never see him again.

As he waited for a break in the traffic, she twisted in her seat to look behind them. She hadn't seen anyone suspicious following her and Lucy, but that didn't mean someone wasn't lurking back there, waiting for the opportunity to make his move. The truth was, she had no idea who would want to kidnap Lucy.

The motive had to be money, because that was the only thing that made sense. She hadn't mentioned how she'd been kidnapped once as a child, after her father had made the news as the first Chicago Billionaire. Granted that was twenty-five years ago, when she was about Lucy's age.

That her daughter would be targeted in the same way, bothered her. She'd cooperated with the police and FBI investigation and had wracked her brain for a list of suspects. But as far as she could tell, the police were no closer to finding this guy.

Which did not bode well for Lucy.

"I'll need your address," Grady said, interrupting her thoughts.

She rattled off the building number then gestured to the skyscraper looming to the right. It looked closer than it actually was. "It's the black building behind that one, it's called Savion Enterprises. We live in the penthouse apartment."

"Underground parking I presume?" He glanced at her.

"Yes." She wasn't sure why Grady made her feel nervous. If anything, it should be the other way around. She was born and raised here in the Windy City of Chicago, but he was a fish out of water. Or he should have been, except that he carried himself with an air of confidence that she envied.

Then again, his child wasn't the intended target of a kidnapping for ransom. She and Lucy were just another job for him. Her father had recommended Grayson's Guardians when she'd asked him for advice. Apparently, Rex Grayson was some sort of war hero who had led a team in combat. A team who all earned bronze stars for their bravery under fire.

She'd jumped at the opportunity of having someone with battle experience protecting her daughter. Now that she was sitting here beside Grady, doubts pummeled her.

He looked competent enough, but she hadn't anticipated his being so—big. Muscular. Rugged. Strong.

She put a hand to her throbbing temple, and told herself to stop being ridiculous. Her lack of sleep was getting to her.

"Are you hungry?" Grady's question caught her by surprise. "I'm happy to stop and grab something if you'd like."

"No thanks. Clara, our housekeeper probably has dinner cooking by now."

"Okay." If he was surprised to hear she had a housekeeper, he didn't show it. "Do you know anything else about the vehicle used in the abduction?"

"The car was a black SUV." His Jeep was black, too. "I believe it was a Honda."

His green gaze flicked to the rear-view mirror, then back at her. "Lots of black SUVs on the road."

Her heart thumped painfully against her sternum. She twisted in her seat again to look through the back window. "Do you see something suspicious?"

"Just stating a fact." His calm demeanor did not make her feel any better. "Traffic is so congested here that it's hard to spot a tail. That's why I was thinking it would be good to stop and get food. See if the two black SUVs behind us stick around or keep going."

"Mom? Is the bad man back there?" The fear underscoring Lucy's tone wrenched at her heart. No child should be afraid of being kidnapped.

"I don't think so, sweetie. Mr.—ah, Grady is just being cautious." She flashed him a pointed look. "Right?"

"Right." Grady made eye contact with her daughter. "Don't worry. Nothing bad is going to happen while I'm around, okay?"

"Okay." Lucy's tremulous smile tugged at her heart. Having divorced Nelson five years ago and obtaining sole custody, her daughter didn't have any memories of her father. Since Nelson was in jail for manslaughter, Lauren preferred to keep it that way. How she'd been so blind to Nelson's dark side, she had no idea.

Maybe it was wrong to be glad Nelson was in jail. Their divorce had been contentious despite the prenup she'd required him to sign. She'd soon learned Nelson had only married her because of her wealth.

Whatever. That was old news. As much as she could easily envision Nelson doing something as low as abducting his own daughter for a hefty ransom, he was in jail. And therefore, couldn't be responsible.

Someone else was behind this. Too bad the list of suspects pretty much included everyone who resented the wealthy.

"I changed my mind. Let's stop for pizza." Once the idea took hold in her mind, she couldn't let it go. She glanced at Grady. "You can have whatever you like, but we need to order one pepperoni pizza for Lucy."

"Really? Pepperoni pizza?" Lucy sounded excited. "Yay!"

A reluctant smile tugged at the corner of her mouth as she glanced back at her daughter. "We'll have to blame Grady for wanting pizza so Clara doesn't get upset with us."

"Oh yeah?" Grady's wry drawl made her glance at him to see if he was truly upset. The twinkle in his green eyes indicated he wasn't. "Sure, make me the bad guy right out of the gate."

"It's just that she fusses over us and takes it personally when we don't eat what she's prepared." Lauren shrugged. "Normally that's not a problem as I prefer to serve Lucy healthy meals."

"Healthy is fine, but this is a special occasion," Grady said. When she frowned in confusion, he rolled his eyes. "Our engagement! Surely you haven't forgotten our engagement already."

She blushed at his teasing. The people around her tended to cater to whatever she wanted. Which quite frankly got old fast. She wasn't used to being teased.

"Of course I didn't forget. That's a great excuse for us to

use." She decided not to point out that if they were truly engaged, they'd be celebrating with steak, lobster and champagne. For a moment she envied Grady's simpler lifestyle. Then gave herself a mental shake. There was no point in wishing for something else. She'd been given many blessings. And she'd made it her mission to champion various charity events. Her favorite by far was the work she did as the spokesperson for Saint Mary's Children's Hospital in Chicago. When Lucy had been born, she'd needed emergency open heart surgery. From that point forward, Lauren had made it her mission to make sure all children received the care they needed, regardless of their ability to pay.

Thankfully, she was in a position to make that happen. Not only where her parents were wealthy but her father's parents had left her a large trust fund. A fund that Nelson had hoped to get his hands on.

The jerk.

"What's your favorite pizza place?" Grady asked, interrupting her thoughts.

"Um." She didn't want to admit that when they ordered pizza, Clara took care of the details.

"I like Captain Jack's pizza," Lucy announced. "That's the kind Ariel's parents get from the store."

Grady shot her a quizzical look, probably wondering what kind of world her daughter lived in. "Any pizza you think looks good is fine with us," she hastily added.

"Got it." He made an abrupt turn to the right. She braced herself with a hand on the dashboard when she heard a loud crack.

Confused, she looked around, wondering if someone had gotten in a car crash.

"Down!" Grady shoved her head down as he drove the

Jeep up and over a curb. The jarring motion made her teeth snap together.

"Mommy?" Lucy's plaintive voice had her turned to look at her daughter. When she noticed the rear window was shattered, she belatedly realized the banging sound wasn't a car crash.

It was gunfire!

www.ingramcontent.com/pod-product-compliance
Lightning Source LLC
Chambersburg PA
CBHW060326310726